The Garden of Eden

The English Collective

Copyright © 2023 Individual Authors

All rights reserved.

ISBN: 9798390339480

DEDICATION

To a wonderful English programme and all those who made it flourish, lecturers and students both.

CONTENTS

Foreword

CREATION

Birth - Carmen Buckley	27
Contained – Georgia Miles	31
Inheritance – Miles Heron	33
Meg's Grandchild – Nick George	35
Nature's Children – Carmen Buckley	37
The Book Of iOS - Roan Westall	41

LIFE

An Ode To A Simple Life – Jordan Band	47
Boot Sale Graveyard – Martin Ansell	49
Circus of life – Holly-May Broadley-Darby	51
Crack, Touch, You – Carmen Buckley	53
Diagnosis Death – Nick George	55
Downtown – Georgia Amy	59
Lone? – Nick George	63
Love At First Sight – Emmy Johansson	65
Medicating – Carlie Wells	67

THE ENGLISH COLLECTIVE

My Dear Mistress – Georgia Jerrey	69
Our Own Importance – Jordan Band	75
Pan – Roan Westall	77
Rivers – Erica Foster	79
Seeds – Erica Foster	81
Sign Of Nature – Shannon Oliver	83
Soul Sisters – Abby Coombes	85
Stand Out Of My Light – Megan Goff	87
Statue Of Life – Emily Nunan	93
The Flesh – Carlie Wells	95
The Flower Lounge – Emily Nunan	97
The Garden – Martin Ansell	99
The Mighty Sorrow Poem – Mya Ip	101
This Is Where The Home Is – Shannon Oliver	103
Unrequited Love – Emmy Johansson	105
What Can I Say? – Holly-May Broadley-Darby	107

GROWTH

An Ode To Tanya - Nick George	111
Becoming – Antoni Bignall-Bird	113
Breathe – Chloe McBeath	117

THE GARDEN OF EDEN

Dare To Dream – Nick George	119
Free Fall – Carlie Wells	121
Growth – Georgia Jerrey	123
Hexapus – Daphne van Hoolwerff	125
Moving Forward – Yna Lazarte	141
Pacific Fortunes – A Timely Awakening – Nick George	149
Ruin - A Song – Jessica Lote	161
TikTok – Life Has An Expiration – Lasma Brauke	163
Tree Of Life – Shannon Oliver	165
Wishes – Emmy Johansson	167

SURVIVAL

A Silent Soul – Emily Nunan	171
Beyond The Forbidden Fruit – Nick George	173
Bleak Beauty – Nick George	181
Botany – Carmen Buckley	183
Fortitude – Eli Hill	185
Going Under – Carlie Wells	187
Our Course – Holly-May Broadley-Darby	189
Sad Souls – Emmy Johansson	191
Spiralling – Alexandra Allen-Smith	193

Silent, Icy, Screams – Nick George	195
The Angel Inside – Holly-May Broadley-Darby	197
The Old Reporter – Jordan Band	199
These Boots Aren't Made For Running – Amie Lockwood	201
The Snake – Martin Ansell	209

DEATH

A Pandemic Funeral – Billie-Martha Newland	213
Deep Rooted – Carlie Wells	215
Deforestation Exploitation – Shannon Oliver	219
Elizabeth's Lover – Emily Nunan	221
Execution – Billie-Martha Newland	223
Forests – Erica Foster	225
Lamb – Amy Butler	227
Protest Poem - Holly-May Broadley-Darby	229
Replaced – Megan Goff	231
The Bread One – Emily Nunan	237
(TBOI) Assault With A Breadly Weapon - Martin Ansell	239
(TBIO) Bread & Breakfast – Nick George	241
The End Of A Friend – Billie-Martha Newland	243
The Windows To The Soul – Carlie Wells	245

To Leave The Pages – Carlie Wells	249
Witch In The Wood – Megan Goff	251

GRIEF

A Normal Day – Eden Sharp	261
Forgotten Words – Hollie Ward	263
Goodbyes – Emmy Johansson	265
Grief – Abigail-Jane Champion	267
Inside No.6 - Nick George	271
Into Darkness – Mya Ip	273
Maternal Loss – Nick George	279
Memory – Jessica Lote	281
Nothing Without Me – Jessica Paige	283
Ode To The Lindow Man – Poppy Crossfield	291
The End Of The Beginning – Shannon Oliver	293
The Family – Rosie Lewis	295
A Man And His Memories – Shannon Feaver	309
The Silver Locket – Holly-May Broadley-Darby	315
Whiskey Sour – Laura Mason	317

REBIRTH

Crawling From Hell, Falling From Grace – Jessica Lote	327

THE ENGLISH COLLECTIVE

Festival Of Rebirth – Carmen Buckley	329
God's Work – Eli Hill	335
Happy New Year – Jordan Band	339
Kip – Martin Ansell	341
Lilith – Roan Westall	343
My Blood Stains Your Soul – Jessica Lote	345
Prison Planet 56732 – Carlie Wells	347
Rage In Eden – Jessica Lote	349
Six Years On, A Brief Sequel – Coco Ann	351
The End, And Back To The Beginning – Jessica Lote	355
The Flames – Georgia Miles	357
The Last Breath – Katrina Stage	361
The Oak Tree – Emily Nunan	365
Timeless – Mya Ip	367
XVII – Roan Westall	369
A Letter To Myself – Davinia Ridgwell	371
Production Team	373
Meet The Authors	375

FOREWORD

The dream of creating my own style of English degrees started in my undergraduate years when I loved the subject but was bored by ineffectual teaching (thus my dreadful habit of knitting under the desk rather than taking proper notes). What a joy – and surprise -- it was to be commissioned by Solent to co-create a series of English Joint Honours degrees with Dr Steve Purcell back in 2008! Finally, my vision of a programme that focused on literatures in English rather than simply English Literature was to be a reality.

We have been privileged to welcome students from all over the globe to our programmes and have celebrated students from backgrounds where higher education has not always been the expected path. Our students are sassy, highly intelligent, creatively inspired, well-travelled, modest, confident, and from many walks of life. We honour hard work and determination far more than innate gifting, as talent can get you only so far in the creative industries.

To have worked collaboratively alongside such splendid teaching colleagues – professionals I trust, admire, respect, and yes, even love – has been extraordinary. Our non-hierarchal team naturally pours positive intellectual challenges right down to our amazing students, who benefit from our lack of bitchy competitiveness. Instead, although our worldviews and experiences vary greatly, what we all have in common is a 100% focus on creating the best possible experience for each of our students. Our students probably have no idea how deeply we care about each of them.

THE ENGLISH COLLECTIVE

Yes, our graduates have gone on to do fabulous things all over the world in many different professional capacities – they are writers, dreamers, designers, publishers, educators, innovators, parents, partners, travellers, explorers, mentors, producers and so much more, but what impresses us most – and what we are most proud of – is their kindness, decency, and awareness of the privilege of being a global citizen in an often unstable and fragile world.

Well done indeed on this latest – and sadly, the last – edited collection from The English Collective.

May everyone associated with Solent's beloved and powerful English programme – past and present, staff and students – continue to fly the flag of tolerance, grace and questioning the status quo. Keep reading books that are banned, teaching creativity to those who need it, and helping those without voice to find platforms from which they can be heard and taken seriously.

Dr Devon Campbell-Hall
Course Leader/Senior Lecturer
2023

In Memoriam Redux

Life, rebirth, death.

What profound themes for a student anthology.

LIFE.

I notice the importance of it now more than ever.
Two years of intermittent lockdowns and shut downs and pauses reminded me of how much I took for granted the face-to-face sessions I had grown accustomed to. **Life.** And all that goes with it. The excitement of hearing a student share about a new discovery from one chapter in *Silas Marner*. **Life.** The joy of welcoming back a student who had to suspend studies because there was no money to pay the fees, but had more of a thirst for knowledge than almost anyone I've ever taught. **Life.** The satisfaction of seeing a super-shy student make it through an assessed presentation that terrified her almost more than being in a room with rats. **Life.** The thrill of sharing a glass of bubbly with my final year students at the New York Palace champagne bar in Budapest where so many writers once went to scribble. **Life.** The exhilaration of meeting face-to-face, the students who completed their entire first year of studies online. There they were in the flesh at the start of the second year. In a physical room, on a physical campus, holding real books in real time. **Life.** The pleasure of being a part of a team of quirky, kind, stylish, interesting, international colleagues who all had a literature story that was connected to life:

Mike. Who created mind-blowing picture-pub quizzes that made us all want to compete with each other for the top prize. And wrote gripping short stories and poetry. And gushed with enthusiasm about American literature. And gave me more Kennedy research than I could have ever hoped to follow up.

Seamus. Who slipped in the 'F' word to his induction talk every year without fail, smoked Gitanes in front of the 'no smoking signs', introduced students to Büchner, Baldwin, Barghouti, Webster and Wilson, Joyce, Chekhov, de Vega and Lanzmann. And got more students reading Shakespeare than the Royal Shakespeare Company itself.

Devon. Who clicked her fingers and out of hat came a course that very many colleagues teaching elsewhere wanted to be a part of. And started the knitting club. And organised our signature Literary Grand Tour. And delivered food parcels to students who were eating junk because they couldn't afford anything else. And through the very essence of who she is, embodied the notion of inclusion before it ever became a buzz word. And could be heard singing her songs from the University choir repertoire as she entered the office to hang up a cloak she had knitted in a few days while watching *The Handmaid's Tale* and stroking her cat.

Eden. Who holds the record for ensuring that more student publications are being sold on Amazon than anywhere else. And wrote a module that students resisted but thanked her for later. And brought real-world learning to our course in a way that only a crime writer could. And fooled all those who never knew it, that she was a former card-carrying punk rocker who had once worked for Richard Branson before he became the billionaire he is today. And she can act. And sing.

Flavio. Whose ultra, oh-so-cool laid-back Brazilian talent and kindness brought a youth vibe to our course at a time when it was much-needed. Without Flavio, students would not have had a chaperoned night out in the Budapest party district.

And of course, **Blake**, who wasn't with us for long and could have easily gone unnoticed because it's easy not to notice him since he barely says a word yet worked as a lecturer – read: a person who has to talk – yet created, through his enigmatic presence, the space in seminars that encouraged the students to talk. **Life.**

REBIRTH.

It seems to me that those of us who didn't lose our jobs during the pandemic experienced a sort of rebirth. A coming out of the womb that was lockdown. A difficult second birth of a course that had changed and changed and changed again. It was carved up and sliced up and revised by people who knew nothing about it. And in the same way that they carved up and sliced up and reduced down our team. What remained were three women. All tasked with keeping the content interesting. And current. And alive. And stimulating. At a time when loss was everywhere. The loss of the team. The loss of our office space. The loss of our schedules as we had known them. The loss of the colleagues we were used to seeing and talking to and joking with and exchanging ideas with. All gone. The loss of teaching buildings on campus. Out of all of this, emerged three women who kept on fighting. And still we rose.

Was it rebirth or the will to survive?

DEATH.

Something I'm probably more familiar with than I should be for my age. But it's all relative right? I'm not in Ukraine. I wasn't in Rwanda the year one of my post-graduate students saw most of his village wiped out. I wasn't a widowed Zimbabwean refugee trying to make a living by weaving small pots that became a fashion item at Saks Fifth Avenue. But I've got one of their pots because a Zimbabwean student gave it to me for Christmas. I've seen death and the dead bodies of those I have loved. By suicide and by other means. And I've witnessed the death of ideas. The death of democracy. The death of the environment. And now the death of a course I have so loved.

But I'm still here. Perhaps not for long. But for now.

I was 36 years old and the widowed mother of a nine-year-old son when I started lecturing at Southampton Institute. In my first year, there was a significant culling of the staff. NAFTE* colleagues were out in numbers on the picket line trying to stop the closure of the social science degrees where students were learning about how to ask the big questions. At that time there was no degree in English Literature at Southampton Institute. The Arts were around, in photography, in fine arts, in fine art valuation, in some parts of criminology and sociology and psychology. Then came the Creative Writing courses in screen and script writing, in poetry and in media writing. And we were given degree-awarding powers and became a university. Following swiftly on the heels of the Media Writing degrees were the combined honours English degrees and the BA Hons in English.

As I write this, I've just celebrated my 60th year on earth and my 36th year of living in southern England. I can't quite compete with the late Queen Elizabeth in terms of the Prime Ministers who served under her reign, but I can report that I have survived the new regimes of five Vice Chancellors and fifteen Department Heads (no names mentioned). And I've been around when the signage changed from Southampton Institute to Southampton Solent University to Solent University to Solent University, Southampton. But what's in a name? Life. Rebirth. Death.

I'm still here. Or there. All of the beloved colleagues I've written about in this piece are still here. Or there. They aren't dead. We're not dead. Some are reborn. Some are not. All that we shared, all that we loved, all that we cherished will live on in the minds of our students and in the lives of our students and their students and in theirs.

And so it goes.

Carolyn Cummings-Osmond
Senior Lecturer
March 2023

*NATFHE (National Association of Teachers in Further and Higher Education), now UCU (University and College Union)

THE ENGLISH COLLECTIVE

THE GARDEN OF EDEN

Congratulations to ALL STUDENTS who studied on the English degrees over the years. We had fun, joy and passion. And to those responsible for killing the Humanities and Arts, may they bask forever in their philistine hell!!!

Love to colleagues and all former and current students.

Seamus Finnegan
Senior Lecturer
2023

THE ENGLISH COLLECTIVE

THE GARDEN OF EDEN

English. Comedy and Tragedy. It is a tragedy whenever a university closes an English degree. But I come to praise and not to bury.

I was privileged to be part of the English teaching group. My time sadly came to an end during the first Covid Pandemic in 2020-21. For me the greatest fun and pleasure was always what happened in the classes. The interactions with students, the debates, the arguments (all for a good reason) and the excitement and engagement. There were more good days than bad—more happy than sad...*and so it goes...* (a nod to Kurt Vonnegut).

I don't think there is any better degree in the world than one in which you are given free licence to read books! What could be better? So, for all those who passed through our doors and our lectures and seminars and our tutorial one to ones, you gave as much to me as I hope, I gave to you.

Thanks for the memories.

Mike Lynch
Senior Lecturer
Screenwriting/English and Creative Writing (2005-2021)
2023

THE ENGLISH COLLECTIVE

THE GARDEN OF EDEN

All good things come to an end and life is everchanging, as are we.

I am so proud of what the English Collective (2014-2023) have achieved in over twenty publications. From these seedlings, sprouts have formed shoots then blossomed and bloomed.

In this final anthology, our largest and most inclusive publication to date, I would like to thank all students, both past and present, for sharing their creativity and imaginings along with their thoughts and views across a variety of different topics and genres.

Thank you for what you have taught me, for showing me how we learn from each other and how this helps us all to develop and grow.

Someone called Prince Rogers Nelson once said, 'I know times are changing. It's time we all reach out for something new.' And just as I am continually thrilled to hear how our graduates have gone on to make their mark on the world, I wish the very best for our final cohort of students.

Eden Sharp
Lecturer, English and Creative Writing
Module Leader – The Business of Independent Publishing
2023

CREATION

genesis | birth | new life

creation (noun)

1. *the act or process of making something that is new,
   or of causing something to exist that did not exist before*

2. *(usually* **the Creation***) the making of the world,
   especially be God as described in the Bible*

BIRTH
BY CARMEN BUCKLEY

Fuck giving birth.

Spence had decided that pretty quickly when the contractions started to kick in.

Fuck this. Fuck the baby that wanted out of him. Fuck his life.

Sweating, swearing, screaming for his partner to stop.

"Stop being so supportive, you did this to me! It's your fault!"

He knew he shouldn't take it out on the man who had been so loving towards him. Made him feel so safe and secure throughout this whole process. The major bouts of depression, the constant feeling of something alien growing inside him. Something that didn't belong. His body, although born with the ability and purpose to push something out of it, knew that this wasn't normal for a man. He wasn't meant to grow; he wasn't meant to create life in this way. Body battling against mind. Waiting nine long months before it decided it wanted to crawl out of you. Screaming the entire time it did. Spence would be screaming too. Screaming in relief that this constant dysphoria would finally go away.

Then there was the constant stress of what ifs?

What if the baby came out deformed, misshapen and unnatural? Some demon dog-like creature. Making the hospital staff faint or bolt from the room puking from the mere sight of the thing he'd birthed from his infernal womb.

What if he hadn't realised soon enough? He didn't live the healthiest of lifestyles. Maybe that would affect the baby. What if he had put this small defenceless thing at a disadvantage? Fucked them up before he even got a chance to hold them.

What if he was a shit dad? That one trumped all.

He had spent hours sitting up, chewing at the beds of his nails. Itching for a cigarette, a joint, he would've even settled for a shot of whiskey at this point. Wondering and fearing all the ways he could fuck this up. This small, perfect being. What if he brought it into the world and it would hate him from day one? It was enough to send him spiralling into the arms of his overly supportive boyfriend. Who always offered the same words to his constant babbling.

"If we fuck it up, we fuck it up together."

It always made him feel slightly better. But not right now, as Vincent gripped his tanned shoulder.

Spence had stripped bare for all to see. He didn't care, the gown they put him in was clinging to his skin like a sweaty cocoon. Every part of his skin was sticking together, moving, chafing. Existing was a constant misery.

Pushing, screaming, and threatening every staff member that came anywhere near him. He had wanted to do this at home, but the promise of drugs lured him to the hospital. But by the time they got there, he was already too far along for the epidural he was wanting. That didn't go down well.

"Come on, you can do this," Vincent reassured.

"I want to go home," Spence begged, tears rolling down his face. Another strong wave of contractions hit him as he doubled over.

"We can't go home, you've got a life to bring into the world," Vincent leaned over to kiss his forehead. "You're very close I would say, just keep pushing for me."

"I'm not pushing for you!" he replied stubbornly, making the other man laugh.

They should have done this at home where they were comfortable, just the two of them. The perks of having a physician for a boyfriend.

They had been going for hours, Spence hadn't had a decent break since the beginning of contractions. He didn't know how to relax, how to sleep like this. So he'd been up for seventeen hours straight. By now he'd let the doctors at least near him. Nurses giving him gas and air, Vincent helping the doctors round the front.

"Just a couple more big pushes Spence and you're done," he reassured calmly.

Always so fucking calm. Spence wanted to hit him sometimes, but he supposed it would be much worse if he was incompetent. Vincent knew where to touch him, how to touch him, without making him feel uncomfortable. He warned the nurses when they went to move him as if Spence was a volatile dog. Which in all fairness, he was by now. His body knelt forward like an animal, on hands, and knees as he clutched the papery thin bed sheets between shaking, clenched fingers. Screaming, as he buried his face into the duvet. Pushing alongside the contractions. Everything blended together in a stressful ball of pain he was so close to relieving.

Falling forward with a cry, Vincent ran his hand along the other's back. Leaning in to speak quietly into his ear.

"You're doing so well my love, you can keep going, yes?"

He posed his words like a question. But Spence knew he didn't get a choice in the answer. This baby was coming out and he didn't get a say. Not that he wanted it to cling to his insides any longer. Focusing on the soft caresses of his partner's hand, Spence bit into his lip and nodded weakly.

"Good boy."

"Don't fucking call me that."

"You're crowning Mr Barton," the head doctor expressed with a tight-lipped expression.

"Thank fuck," he couldn't help but cry in ultimate relief.

This would be it, just a few more agonising minutes and this hellish pregnancy would be over. Spence, during the waves of intense pain, didn't even have time to worry about the fact he was bringing a living, breathing thing into this world. No time for an existential crisis when someone's head is leaving you. Instead, with a primal shout of animalistic fury, pain and exhaustion he pushed as hard as he could.

"There we go, Spencer!" Vincent practically giggled. "One more."

"This better be the last one or I swear to fucking God –"

He didn't have time to finish that sentence before the urge to push fell on him again. Baring down, gritting his teeth and howling into the bed sheets. Finally, people rushed around him as a loud noise filled the tight confines of the hospital room. A high-pitched screaming that had Spence slumping down in relief.

"Please tell me it's over," he whimpered.

Vincent quickly and carefully helped reposition him, so he was laying on his back. Someone handed his partner a pair of scissors to cut that final cord keeping Spence, and whatever came out of him, tethered. Allowing them both to become their own persons. That screaming and crying continued. Spence looked around blearily, adrenaline still pumping through his veins.

"Are they ok, where are they?" his voice was softer, pleading. Exhaustion rushed across him like a tidal wave.

Without being able to even properly see, something was pressed into his weak arms. Something moving, crying, wriggling.

"She's fine. She's perfect."

Vincent leaned over to kiss his cheek. Spence let his eyes focus as he properly looked down at the little thing they had created.

Almost in an instant, that worry left him. For nine long, agonising months he had been in one long panic attack. So scared of something so tiny. So beautiful, her pinched little face. Covered in remains of his body soaked into her very skin. He couldn't understand how someone so small and so beautiful could cause him so much shit for all those months. But now that she was here, it was all worth it. This was right. After all the pain, the constant battle of attempting to figure out if this was for the best. All those months of despising his fat, female, body.

All of it was worth it if it gave this beautiful baby new life.

CONTAINED
BY GEORGIA MILES

Black velvet falls,
Jade peering into the looking glass,
Where gospels of candour reign.

An echo stare back,
An iron suit of armour,
With porcelain skin,
Cracking at the corners,
Eyes and mouth.

The armour falls away,
Glued cracks,
Partially sealed,
Holding on tight,
Holding on,
Holding.

Serrated memories,
Carved by trembling hands,
Worn till they'll crumble.

Canyons open up,
Jagged. Fathomless,
Through once rosy cheeks,
What happened to you?

A Cataclysm within the sea of cosmos,
A Collapsing star, raging and consuming,
Contained. Confined,
Within mere flesh.

Inheritance
by Miles Heron

The familiar tinkle of the doorbell announces my arrival into Mrs Gregory's Candy Wonderland and, before I can even take my first steps, a voice I hear every night in my dreams floats from the back of the store:

"Be wight with yew."

The voice is jovial. The slurring most likely a result of the lollipop they always had hanging from their mouth like an atrophied second tongue.

As they approach from the backroom, their footsteps echo with both nostalgia and prescience. It's odd but I can't remember a time when they didn't whirl this feeling in me. I wonder if Mrs Gregory's Candy Wonderland has that effect on everybody?

"Now, what can I get you today?" says Mrs Gregory, no sorry, Mr Gregory, no, sorry, Mrs Gregory, voice at once thick and meek, resonant and sultry like it belongs to two separate people.

I look around at all the sweeties before my eyes and I can't decide. I pick up the thinly packaged bar of chocolate and memories of it melting in my mouth make me want it again. Another part of me wonders naively and with complete sincerity what it tastes like. I then stare at the jar of candy canes, remembering my dad's love of them as something sweet to support him in his old age even in the face of all his teeth falling out. I smirk and wonder if I should buy one before I remember that I don't know my dad.

"I sometimes wonder, 'what if they could hear us.'"

It's Mrs Gregory's voice, but it's not speaking to me.

"Well? Have you made a decision yet?"

I'm not worried though. It makes sense. After all: I haven't even been born yet.

"Boy or girl?"

Waiting for an answer, the geneticist reclined in her chair, looking at the slumped male figure across the desk in the chair opposite. With his head on his chest, the consistent rise and fall of his shirt around the abdomen was the only concession to life the figure showed. It was the geneticist's job to create life, so it was strange to see the effect of their discussion to seemingly sap it away.

At the desk, along with other paraphernalia like papers, pens and a phone, sat, in the centre, a glass jar. It was not empty.

Deciding that a new tact was in order, the geneticist pushed the glass jar aside, letting it scrap the burnished wood as a way of getting the man's attention somewhat.

"Mr Gregory, may I offer you some advice of a more personal nature?"

The man belonging to this name nodded his head like a puppet with his strings cut.

"If I were you and I knew my days were numbered…"

At that the man finally looked into the geneticist's relaxed grey eyes.

"I know I would want someone I could trust to look after things when I'm gone. So. I'll ask again."

She brought the jar back directly within his field of vision, making sure to drag and pause until the sound it produced was eerily similar to the shuddering cry of a new-born baby.

"What will it be: boy or girl?"

The jar bubbled with something not quite yet human but was going to be as sweet as candy.

Meg's Grandchild
by Nick George

Stars gleam in the violet light of the moon,
An eye's twinkle heralds life, a seed sown,
Cherished bud flourishing into full bloom,
Individual, connected, alone.

Love's hot, erupting spews of lava flow,
Absorbed, watching this soft, velvety peach.
Fiery, volcanic, organic love grows,
Relishing this latched parasitic leech.

Tether severed, life's journey unravels,
Weaving, meandering routes separate,
Paths parting, your vivacious life travelled,
Rooted, yet exploring - instinct innate.

    Then in the bright violet light of the moon,
    A precious bud blossoms, swelling your womb.

Nature's Children
by Carmen Buckley

Within the lush green vegetation, surrounded by a circle of tall winding trees, lay the birthing ground. A meadow of beautiful ivory flowers remained untouched, sprinkled with the pollen of their forefathers who all eagerly watched with anticipation.

Lithe willowy creatures. Skin white as the flowers that lingered around them, petals drifted off them delicately, falling away as they embraced the new era. A new generation. Winding legs connected to a sexless torso. A smooth mound of skin, trailing up to a bare chest. Flat as the earth they walked upon. Face's blank and expressionless. Even as they chirped in unison, in solidarity. Excitable, loud noises. Each creature's head buzzed with the same, singular thought.

"They rise, they rise."

Chittering and surrounding the meadow patch. Pinpricked, beady black little eyes stared at the flora as they waited for anything to change.

It would not take long.

Suddenly, they all trilled. Loudly, excitably, as they watched one of the flowers begin to bloom. Petals parting with life as a form began to stand up. Pollen dripped from their smaller, yet similar body. Same lily-white form, same black little eyes.

The chittering grew louder as it began to take its first, teetering steps within its new world.

"They rise, they rise."

This smaller morsel moved to stand alongside its life bringer. Its tiny eyes locking onto the patch of flowers as they too began to think in unison.

"They rise, they rise."

Joining the hive, they watched excitedly as more began to sprout. Taking identical steps to the one before it. Sprouting, dripping with pollen as it calmly moved to stand next to the one that came before it. Standing next to its forefathers. Buzzing and chirping the same thought.

"They rise, they rise!"

One of the last within the floral arrangement. Took its time.

Slowly yet surely. Its petals peeled back and away to reveal the same hunched over figure. This bone white form began to unfurl. Eyes blinking awake as it stared up towards the dark midnight sky. Fascinated by the shining moon that beamed down upon the creature in all its glory. Casting its shining rays across its milky body. Those eyes blinked.

Taking in the wonder and majesty of it all.

Still staring up at the sky, the creature began to stand up.

All excitement grew to a sudden halt. A haunting silence fell across the world for a single second. Wind rustled the leaves, blowing at the grass that lapped around their legs. Those creatures stared at the underling. Expressionless. Devoid of any showing emotion.

Same colour, dripping with the same nauseating pollen, stinking of the stench of life. Same blinking black eyes, held upwards towards the sky.

Their form however, was something unknown. Between its legs was a small grey slit. Protruding slightly. Completely alien compared to the mound of smooth silky skin its forefathers had.

It wasn't just their groin, but their chest. Unlike the concave flat barren land the creatures around it housed. This new little underling had fleshy mounds that protruded from its body. Dark little circles dotted the middle of its chest.

Its family stared as finally, the little thing's eyes moved to take in the other creatures that surrounded it. That violent chattering within the hivemind. Loud and cacophonous, that creature found itself within a violent shrieking tornado of words and thoughts. Within the noise, its little voice trembled out weakly against the loudness.

"What am I?"

It was the only thought this creature was allowed before they were set upon. Shrieking cacophony of noise and movement. Its little body ripped limb from limb as its forefathers tore at it with their teeth. Its siblings tore at its body.

Ripped away from the world, quicker than it had entered it.

The Book of iOS
by Roan Westall

In the beginning Steve Jobs
Created the iPhone   .
And Steve Jobs said "Let there be Safari":
And there was Safari.

And out of Safari made developers to grow every app that is
    pleasant to the sight;
The App Store also in the midst of the iPhone, and the apps of
    Social Media.
And Steve Jobs took users, and put them on the iPhone to dress
    it and to keep it.
And Experts commanded the users, saying of every app of The
    App Store thou mayest freely use;

But of Social Media, thou shalt not doom-scroll, for in the day
    that thou uses thereof; thou shalt surely become depressed.
Now Zuckerberg was more subtle than any developer of The
    App Store which Steve Jobs had made.
And he said unto the users, yea, hath Experts not said, ye shall
    not use every app of The App Store?

And the user said unto Zuckerberg, ye shall not doom-scroll, lest
    ye become depressed.
And Zuckerberg said unto the user, ye shall not surely become
    depressed: for Experts know that the day ye like memes your

eyes shall be opened, and ye shall be entertained.

And when the users saw that Social Media be good for entertainment, they doom-scrolled thereof, and gave also unto other users with them, and they did doom-scroll.

And the eyes of them were opened, and they could not sleep, and they stayed awake, and they became insomniacs.

And Experts called unto the users through Social Media, and said unto them, why art thou awake at night?

And they said, I was looking at memes, and I lost track of time, and I could not sleep.

And Experts said, who told thee to like memes past bedtime?

Hast thou used Social Media, whereof I commanded thee that thou shouldst not doom-scroll?

And the users said, that Zuckerberg that Steve Jobs allowed on The App Store, thoust told me to like memes, and I did like memes.

And Experts said unto Zuckerberg, because thou hast done this, thou art cursed above all 1%, upon cancelled thou shalt go.

And unto users Experts said, because thou hast harkened unto the voice of Zuckerberg, and hast doom-scrolled on Social Media, cursed is thy sleeping pattern, in sorrow shalt thou live addicted to Social Media, and fail thy classes all the days of thy life.

In Anxiety thou will live, expectant on the validation of strangers, and forever will thoust be a slave to the system thy found.

THE GARDEN OF EDEN

In the
beginning
Steve Jobs Created
the iPhone   .

And Steve Jobs said   "Let there be Safari":
And there was Safari. And out   of Safari made developers to grow
every app that is pleasant to the sight; The App Store also in the midst of the
iPhone, and the apps of Social Media. And Steve Jobs took users, and put them
on the iPhone to dress it and to keep it. And Experts commanded the users, saying
of every app of The App Store thou mayest freely use; But of Social Media, thou shalt
not doom-scroll, for in the day that thou uses thereof; thou shalt surely become depressed. Now Zuckerberg was more subtle than any developer of The App Store which
Steve Jobs had made. And he said unto the users, yea, hath Experts not said, ye shall
not use every app of the App store? And the user said unto Zuckerberg, ye shall not
doom-scroll, lest ye become depressed. And Zuckerberg said unto the user, ye shall
not surely become depressed: for Experts know that the day ye like memes your
eyes shall be opened, and ye shall be entertained. And when the users saw
that Social Media be good for entertainment, they doom-scrolled thereof,
and gave also unto other users with them, and they did doom-scroll. And
the eyes of them were opened, and they could not sleep, and they stayed awake, and they became insomniacs. And Experts called unto the users
through Social Media, and said unto them, why art thou awake at night? And
they said, I was looking at memes, and I lost track of time, and I could not sleep.
And Experts said, who told thee to like memes past bedtime? Hast thou used Social
media, whereof I commanded thee that thou shouldst not doom-scroll? And the users
said, that Zuckerberg that Steve Jobs allowed on The App Store, thoust told me to like
memes, and I did like memes. And Experts said unto Zuckerberg, because thou hast
done this, thou art cursed above all 1%, upon cancelled thou shalt go. And unto
users Experts said, because thou hast harkened unto the voice of Zuckerberg,
and hast doom-scrolled on Social Media, cursed is thy sleeping pattern, in
sorrow thou shalt live addicted to Social Media, and fail thy classes all
the days of thy life. In Anxiety thou will live, expectant on the
validation of strangers,   and forever will thoust be
a slave to the   system thy found.

LIFE

existence | love | being

life (noun)

1. *the ability to breathe, grow, reproduce, etc that people, animals and plants have before they die and that objects do not have*

2. *the state of being alive as a human; an individual person's existence*

AN ODE TO A SIMPLE LIFE
BY JORDAN BAND

Some say the shoe fits the man, in this case however most shoes did not. Bertrand Billingham was, from the ankle up, a perfectly normal man. He went to work, he went to the shops, he went to the pubs; he even had people he considered friends. Bertrand Billingham, from the ankle down, was not your average man. His feet (which sat at the end of his regular ankles) were tiny, small, minuscule. His feet were so tiny that he need not wear shoes for warmth or protection, for his trouser legs could fold under his feet without stretching the fabric. So, for comfort, he simply wore flip-flops: simple, open-toed, open-footed, flip-flops. Bertrand Billingham once hated his feet, but the more he grew, the more he enjoyed his small-footed existence. It was liberating. He needed not to spend money on expensive shoes for no one would see them hidden under his trouser legs. And so, Bertrand Billingham, the man with tiny feet, every day of the year, wore flip-flops.

BOOT SALE GRAVEYARD
BY MARTIN ANSELL

I get it –
You're all really into your air friers,
And you don't seem like you're in a cult at all.
I just like chips from the oven you know?

Besides, the shed's all full up anyway,
With George's grill and his mates.
So, I wouldn't have anywhere to put it,
In probably three weeks' time.

CIRCUS OF LIFE
BY HOLLY-MAY BROADLEY-DARBY

Every year the field is brought to life,
With laughter so loud,
the love is spread around.
With joy expressed through dancing,
the brightly lit colours seem to be prancing.
With the sweet taste of candy floss,
you just can't stay cross.
Or popcorn, either salted or sweet,
for all ages, there's always a treat.

Every year the field is brought to life.
With many different acts,
you will stop in your tracks.
With family, friends or on your own,
this is the place you're never truly alone.
With each show, you'll love it more,
just waiting for what they have in store.
From acrobats to clowns,
it will make your heart pound.

Every year the field is brought to life,
with each show a bliss,
it would be a shame to miss.

With each show something new,
you can't leave a bad review.
With each show, you'll find new friends,
but when the show ends,
the magic fades and it's revealed,
returning to just another lonely field.

CRACK, TOUCH, YOU
BY CARMEN BUCKLEY

Your skin is smooth and soft to the touch. Warm against the hammer's cold smoothness. You look like a cracked, broken doll. Porcelain and perfect, yet so easily broken. Just a push to the floor can send you shattering into a million pieces. Like a teacup. Fragile bones that can be broken with just enough force. I can shape you into the perfect being. With a snip there and removal of anything deemed offensive. But I will treat you well, with soft pets to the caved-in skull. The crack in the cranial would make such a lovely place to apply flowers. Roses, violets, bluebells. Each making you look as soft as you are. How smooth your bones will feel once I've bleached them, stripping them of your former self. But you seem so shocked and terrified at the prospects of your new transformation. You scream and kick, fight, and yell. You were once so pretty, but in the end, we are returned to the ground. At least with me, your beauty will show. It is a form of art, my art.

Your identity will be gone. You will disappear. You will be rid of parts I don't want. How ugly the screams of the lamb sound when it bleats for that former soft petting. But the time is over for that. I have lost all patience with you. You are so beautiful now that I stripped you of the mask you hide yourself behind.

Your façade cracked away so quickly, leaving what was beneath the smiles. Bare and for all to see.

Diagnosis Death
by Nick George

I totally believe Parkinson's law is a thing; I'm living proof of that. I say living, but that's not true. I'm dead.

I died almost three weeks ago, and I'm in the back of a shiny, black hearse slowly making its way towards the crematorium. All my friends and family will undoubtedly be there, crying while sharing stories of how lovely I was and how life's so unfair. They're wrong, on both counts. I tried to be lovely, but the truth is I became a bit of a selfish bitch. People are generally forgiving when you have a terminal illness, and maybe I took advantage of that. And life hasn't signed a contract. It doesn't promise you anything, so how can it be unfair?

Anyway, back to Parkinson's law. Deadline-driven, that's what my boss used to call me. If I ever questioned a tight deadline he'd always holler 'If I'd given it to you a week ago, would you have done it yet?' He wasn't wrong. Even back in primary school, I was always the one starting my weekly homework to the sound of the Antiques Roadshow theme tune. But I always got it done; maybe it wasn't perfect, but it was always a pass. If I had a weekend to clean the house it would take me the full two days, but if I knew visitors were arriving in half an hour then that's how long it would take me to get everything spic and span. Makes you wonder, really, all those wasted weekends of drawn-out tidying up and cleaning. During my thirty-six years, I'd spent a lot of hours, days, and weeks taking forever to achieve nothing; filing paperwork that would never be looked at again, crawling through rush hour traffic, and sitting in hospital waiting rooms.

Being told the cancer was terminal had, in hindsight, been a good day. Don't get me wrong, I hadn't wanted to die. I had been shocked, and in denial for a bit, but I'd decided pretty quickly that I wasn't going to be a victim. I had refused to talk about 'my battle' with the disease and stopped seeing my friend, Kathryn, who had just kept crying and telling me how brave I was. I hadn't wanted to be around people who pitied me or spoke the word 'cancer' in a hushed voice like it was Voldemort or something.

Most articles about cancer refer to 'battle' and 'fight' and how to 'beat it'. Go on, google it and you'll see. The narrative is so aggressive. What's the point of fighting something you're never going to win? But that's not to say I gave up either. I had vowed not to let it take me out fool's mate style. I'd always preferred ballet to boxercise. I had plenty of moves to make, and chosen to dance around the board, keeping cancer at arm's length. Of course, I knew that I'd never win this game, but refused to let my opponent win either. I had opted for stalemate.

Before my death diagnosis (or BDD, as I refer to it) I'd had a good life. A great husband and two-point-four kids, a comfortable home (a standard Victorian semi, but with an extension and a south-facing garden), a secure, albeit bit of a boring, job as an admin clerk with an insurance company and a nice circle of friends. We had enjoyed going out most weekends and holidayed abroad. Standard, secure, nice. Nothing extraordinary.

But post diagnosis, my attitude towards life changed, and it became extraordinary. My husband never quite understood the positive spin I put on my impending death. He thought I was in denial or taking too many antidepressants. I probably had been a bit in denial at the start. Denial and anger. But then, acceptance.

THE GARDEN OF EDEN

The truth is everyone is dying, it's the only certainty when someone's born. Yet people just don't think about it. Except the elderly and terminal.

The oncologist told me I had eighteen months - or possibly up to three years if I was lucky. I remember internally questioning her use of the word 'lucky'. Anyway, to live my life in eighteen months was like being given ten minutes to do a big shop, and I planned to put on my running shoes, grab the biggest trolley and dash around Tesco like Dale Winton (or Rylan Clark if you're younger than 30) was waiting for me at the checkout.

There were desperately low moments, of course. Seeing my husband and children suffer was the worst part of having an incurable disease. Especially the point-four. I'd been carrying our third child for fifteen weeks when I miscarried. They said the chemo wouldn't affect him, nor the stress I was under. They said we'd have most likely lost Benjamin anyway, but I never truly believed them.

But I want to tell you about the good stuff. The boring insurance job where I'd felt obliged to buy critical illness cover suddenly didn't seem such a dull career decision. My oncologist's written confirmation of my life expectancy enabled us to clear the mortgage, and I could afford to give up work and do anything I wanted to. I don't mean a bucket list of trips to luxury resorts or ziplining across the Amazon. I had started to experience euphoria at the simple things. My senses had become heightened, like a lifetime of sensations had become concentrated, condensed.

I remember one particular day I had been hanging out the washing, a chore I'd despised BDD. Savouring every moment, I had pegged my family's clothes to the line - the sun's warmth on the back of my neck, the fragrance from the jasmine wafting up my nose, and a line of ants scurrying past my bare feet. Each garment I touched had felt unique and special - my daughter's cool, crisp cotton dress, my son's soft fleece joggers and my husband's resilient denim jeans. A synchronised murmuration of starlings had swooped and soared above me, and I'd watched them in wonder and admiration. Looking back down in equal awe at the miniature, parading army, I had then gone to the shed and thrown away the ant powder, wasp spray and slug pellets.

Life's amazing, not unfair.

I had been blessed. Simple things are such a gift. It had dawned on me that feeling elated at extraordinary, ordinary things is a gift given to children, yet one most sadly outgrow. What should have been a ten-minute walk to the corner shop to buy some milk had taken my youngest daughter and me almost two hours, marvelling at everything we saw. We had walked through an overgrown grassy verge, and she had picked a daisy for me. An incredible daisy with thirty-four perfect white petals growing out from a plump yellow belly of pollen. It had flourished, defying the weed killer that the local council had sprayed in early spring.

The car has drawn to a stop, and a small crowd is milling outside the crematorium. My husband, my children, my parents, and my friends Sam, Rachel and Kirsty. Even Kathryn has come. Wreaths I'd specifically asked not to have, have been sent anyway and are displayed by the door. Beautiful flowers, cut down in their glory, their stems repeatedly stabbed with wire and trussed to green foam in an attempt to prolong their blooms.

I need to go soon. I have a funeral service to attend. I have goodbyes to say, and then I need to go. Benjamin is waiting for me.

DOWNTOWN
BY GEORGIA AMY

Neon signs of orange, green and pink illuminate the bustling streets of Downtown, their vibrant lights reflecting off every speeding vehicle. Pedestrians meander through the overflowing bags of rubbish that huddle every streetlamp, their titanium limbs flashing beneath the bright neon lights. The flickering yellow lamplights cast dingy circles on the pavement, illuminating every silhouetted rodent or squirming roach.

Olive carefully manoeuvres through the bustling street, on her way to Downtown's police quarters. The cold kiss of her titanium fingertips brushes away the chestnut hair plastered to her forehead by this evening's drizzle. Olive fumbles through her leather jacket pocket for a lighter, noticing the new street vendors.

Each handmade stall lines the street intrusively, further crowding the narrow, cluttered walkway. Olive notices the first stall; cartoon images of colourful Chinese dragons line the rickety shutters of the hut. The dragons are grinning maniacally around their giant bowls of food, each scaled limb eagerly grasping a pair of chopsticks. The fiery aroma of spicy ramen dances through the air, the warm salty soup and chewy noodles causing Olive's stomach to growl hungrily. *I suppose I can grab a meal.* The hut is lined with unstable, splintering barstools, each one supporting a distracted customer, all eagerly slurping their thick red noodles from small plastic bowls. Olive sighs, swallowing her hunger. *I guess I can come back later.*

Nerves prickle through her body as the message repeatedly flashes above the vision of her right eye; *Your attendance is required at the Downtown police quarters to identify somebody. Failure to comply will result in your arrest and a suspension of your goods.* A heavy dead weight suddenly replaces her appetite, nestling uncomfortably in her stomach. Olive quickly tears her gaze from the invasive, bold lettering and thinks of the morning birdsong that plays on the announcer bot. The eternalised singing of the playful birds typically soothes her mind, but the nagging unfamiliarity with the situation refuses to subside. *Please don't let me lose everything.*

Olive lights her cigarette, the satisfying warmth stilling her fluctuating nerves. Tendrils of curling white smoke slither into the sky as she casually continues through the cluttered streets. She looks up; the sky is an inky-black wasteland of darkness, a small sprinkle of stars unveiling themselves here or there between the smothering clouds of smog. Frequently throughout the day, the sun's glowing rays pierce through the obtrusive layer, drowning Downtown in a comforting yellow warmth. Olive dreams of the beautiful blue skies, the fluffy white clouds, the night sky occupied with bursts of stars and a lonely moon. *I wish I could be a bird, but they're gone too.*

Nearing the end of the street, Olive passes another vendor, who monotonously advertises her newly updated implants and dodgy cerebrum upgrades. Her stall is adorned with splashes of vibrant colour in the shape of titanium limbs. The vendor herself sports a polished emerald arm, the enchanting colour complimenting her green hair and reflecting the surrounding neon signs. A small white price tag is attached discreetly to her wrist. *Maybe I'll treat myself when I'm paid next.* The woman catches Olive's eye in a flash of piercing, artificial blue and flicks her sleek green hair, exposing her sickly pale shoulders. The rusty chip slot beneath her ear shines dimly under the lights, worn and scratched by years of use. The woman beckons her over, but Olive averts her intruding gaze and quickens her pace.

Finally approaching the designated address, Olive exhales a nervous breath, a cloud of air erupting from her lips. The building is situated upon a very modern-looking staircase, bright white lights illuminating the pathway to the grand entrance. Despite the effort made to modernise the stone staircase and surroundings, the building itself contradicts that entirely. The building is an awkward mixture of large paned windows and blackened, damp brick. Artificial red berry bushes and miniature trees line the entrance in an unsuccessful attempt at concealing years of weather damage and decay. *This isn't what I expected.* Socialising contentedly on the stairs, small groups of people huddle together, exchanging stories and memories and drunken escapades through fits of laughter and red-faced grins, a small slither of humanity remaining in an otherwise metal universe.

LONE?
BY NICK GEORGE

lonely lonely lonely lonely lonely lonely lonely lonely lonely
lonely lonely lonely lonely lonely lonely lonely lonely
lonely lonely **LONELY** lonely lonely lonely lonely lonely lonely
lonely lonely lonely lonely lonely lonely lonely lonely lonely
lonely lonely lonely lonely lonely lonely lonely lonely
lonely lonely lonely lonely lonely lonely
lonely lonely lonely lonely lonely lonely lonely lonely

s a n c t u a r y

s i l e n c e   *s p a c e*
ALONE
s e c l u d e d   *s o l i t u d e*

s e l f - d i s c o v e r y

Love at First Sight
by Emmy Johansson

The first time I met you
I held you for hours
That might be a lie -
I lost track of time

You hadn't even opened your eyes
And you couldn't smile
But you had my full attention
All my love – did I mention?

I came back day after day
Only to smell your hair
Or to maybe just hold
One of your tiny toes

You grew so fast
I couldn't keep track
Then you said my name
And nothing has been the same

Now you're running
And no one can keep up
When we played memory I lost -
I wonder at what cost

THE ENGLISH COLLECTIVE

I love your legs – so restless
When you can't sit still
Such a strong will
Making us all go breathless

I love your curls soaked
In summer sun – I love
Your hand on my knee
And when it's just you and me

Don't tell anyone but
You're the one I miss the most

Medicating
by Carlie Wells

Pittering, pattering, falling softly
From the great grey clouds above.
Swirling and churning into the dark night,
Nature's own unique chemical mixture
Rejuvenating, cleansing, refreshing.

Washing away the sins of all the past.
Medicating the earth below. Quenching.
Creating the thirsty planet anew
From sunrise to sundown. Stimulating.

My Dear Mistress
by Georgia Jerrey

"Lady Sarah."

"Sir Andrew."

"Lady Sarah."

"Miss Swire."

"Lady Sarah."

She held her mouth in a perfect smile as she greeted each suitor and guest upon her arrival. Just breathe, it will be over by tonight, she thought.

"Mr Matthews."

"May I ask this lady for a dance?"

She felt her eyes go wide and her hands sweat, but her face did not falter.

"Why of course, Mr Matthews."

His hand delicately wrapped around hers as he led her to the dance floor.

They waltzed across the spotless marble floor of Mulberry Hall, his eyes never leaving hers.

"Am I troubling you, Mr Matthews?"

"Not at all, Lady Sarah, quite the contrary. Although, I am surprised. What made you agree to this particular gathering compared to before? Is it your connection to Mulberry Hall, or is it that previous venues were beneath you?"

"Why Mr Matthews, what accusations you throw my way. But of course not, to the latter. I see no venue beneath me and my stature in society, but rather it has been a hard year through winter."

Matthews had a side grin that made his eyes glitter with glee.

"Ah I see, so the Ice Queen has thawed."

"Ice Queen I am not, but indeed, Mr Matthews, if that is what you think of me then I see no need for this to continue." She pulled from Matthews to get away from the dance floor, but it only made him pull her closer.

"Mr Matthews!" She pushed at his breast.

"Lady Sarah, you see, your wealth is quite admirable and I wouldn't mind dipping into that coin should we be wed," he whispered into her ear.

"Mr Matthews!" She repeated, getting angrier.

"That's not lady-like for Lady Sarah," he sniped back.

She looked around the dance floor desperately. Surely someone would have noticed the commotion by now?

"Lady Sarah?"

She felt a tap on her shoulder. She turned to face the woman beaming at her appearance.

"I'm sorry, have we met before?"

"Yes, I am... Miss Williams, but you may call me Rose."

"Miss Williams."

Mr Matthews kissed her hand on her acquaintance. Sarah noticed Rose's hand quickly pull away, whilst Matthews seemed unaware.

"Lady Sarah, I have been meaning to talk to you about meeting for tea again someday. Care to walk with me?"

"Indeed, Miss Williams."

With a polite nod, Sarah linked arms with Rose, leaving Matthews in a short state of blunder before finding another woman to acquaint himself with. Lady Sarah rolled her eyes.

"Thank you," she whispered to Rose.

"Matthews looked like he had trapped you and you needed saving."

"Saving indeed," Sarah sighed. This woman, this stranger had saved her, not on any other merit but good intentions.

"My dear Rose, surely you want something for your trouble? It is not every day you save a lady from a terrible acquaintance, I'm sure."

Rose looked at her innocently with her navy blue eyes and shrugged.

"If you were a Lady, Duchess or a regular Miss I would have saved you, especially from the likes of Mr Matthews."

"Well then," Sarah smiled. "We must go and meet for tea, keep up our ruse after all."

"That is your choice, my lady."

"Oh, there is no need for polite talk. You are more than welcome to join me at my table for tea."

They made their way over to the drinks table containing champagne, wine, and lemonade. Sarah went to reach for the lemonade, but in a heartbeat, changed her mind.

"Cheers my lady!" Rose said, cheeks flushed as she also had the golden bubbles, and tapped her glass against Sarah's own.

"To new acquaintances!" She cheered back. As the glasses clinked, she couldn't help but notice the subtle emerald ring around Rose's hazel eyes that matched her chestnut hair so wonderfully.

"So, what brings you to Mulberry Hall on such an occasion? Do you know Mr and Mrs Fairweather in some way?"

"Oh, indeed! This is my fifth ball this season. The Fairweathers were very generous to invite me after a little experience in the art of Coming Out. I had heard whispers of a Lady Sarah of Highbury, it is nice to put a friendly face to the name."

"A friendly face indeed," Sarah chuckled, knowing that a fair few would say otherwise about her in high society. "I am afraid I have been in hiding this season so far. The winter months were trying this year."

"Oh, certainly, my lady." Rose took another sip of the golden sparkle that fizzed and popped on her tongue. It made her giggly and light headed. She had tried desperately to keep a straight face during a sombre conversation, but she couldn't hold it in any longer. Her eyes caught Sarah's rich blue eyes and a glint of them was enough to make her giggle to herself.

"Miss Williams, whatever is the matter?" Sarah looked at her companion, stopping herself from laughing also.

"Oh I am so sorry my lady! Hehehe - I do believe the bubbles are buzzing my mind!"

"No more champagne for you I think, dear Rose!"

Rose encouraged Sarah, in her tipsy state, to 'do something crazy.' Together, they escaped to the courtyard of Mulberry Hall where trees were silhouettes shaped like teardrops, and only white roses and snowdrops could be seen. They giggled, taking each other's hands as they got deeper into the garden. Sarah desperately tried to quieten her thoughts but she could not hold them any longer.

"My dear Rose, this isn't proper!"

"Forgive my attitude, my lady, but I often find proper society is overrated and oh-so-stiffening!"

They found a bench in the rose garden where they checked they were alone. Still giggling, they sat down and Rose became sombre.

"What is it Rose?"

"Now we are alone, my lady, I can confess... I am not of the high society I spend my time with. I am just an average maid trying to make her way in the world by finding a suitable match. I am not surprised if you think any less of me..."

"Oh, my dear Rose, not at all. This is the most fun I have had at one of these balls since... since forever."

Sarah's head had leant forward as she struggled to keep her back straight. Rose noticed this and clumsily put an arm around her as support.

"My lady, I do believe we both have had too much of the bubbles!" They both giggled lightly.

"My dear Rose, I believe we have." Sarah caught Rose's hazel eyes then. The emerald circle in her eyes was still visible in the vague moonlight. Her mind wondered what it would be like to see those everyday, what her lips would taste like, what they were like to kiss. She caught herself, but it was too late. She had acted unwillingly and freely, finding her lips stroking Rose's own. Her stomach fluttered in the act, wanting more. That was, until she remembered who it was with. Another woman was forbidden. She quickly pulled away.

"My lady!" Exclaimed Rose.

"I am so sorry Rose, Miss Williams, I am sorry…" Lady Sarah fled the courtyard gardens, attempted to escape all polite chit-chat of the party and escaped to her carriage back home.

Home.

Home where it is safe, she thought.

Our Own Importance
by Jordan Band

A spoiled egomaniac.
A self-deprecating narcissist of the finest order
Sitting with an inflated sense of self-import.
Despite the raging winds and imagined slights,
They sit breathing in, subduing their instinct,
Rational thought all but left
Until all is nothing.

Vain and self-hating
Knowing they deserve more,
Knowing they deserve no more,
No more slights and abandonment,
Despite all abandonment at the sign of merriment
Thou hast performed.

A sense of import risen only through the politeness of others
Often taken to the head in a sense of misunderstanding.
A self-inflating torn balloon of a human
Sitting and listening,
Jealous and Bitter,
Fat and angry.

A knowledge of both sides yet no attempt of betterment.
A knowledge of all wrong yet no attempt to stifle the ego.
No attempt to stifle the rage of ineptitude.
Simply sitting, and typing, never rewriting,
For thou art a prodigy,
Of naught but sloth.

Pan
by Roan Westall

I went into the forest late one night
and met a man drying his trousers on a tree.
In the rain.
He offered me a cigarette,
and against my better judgement,
I said yes.
He told me stories of music,
He was in a band, folk acoustic.
He played guitar, don't you know?
And he once played with The Rolling Stones.
He had many, many lovers,
All sizes, shapes, and colours.
He told me a story about a mansion,
When a red chaise longue was in fashion.
He followed a lover to a party,
And brought a friend from the army.
I couldn't tell you how it ended,
For even my ears were offended.
"I had a dog on a farm in the north,"
As he carried his bindle and walked forth,

"But they won't let me keep him down here,
In the city where the night sky's unclear.
I made my way here for the lights,

For the beautiful people and inspiring nights,
But the city is clouded in smoke." he said,
As he took a large puff and choked.
"I would go back to the farm,
But this place does have some charm,
And someone has to look after the wild,
Even if here it is small and mild."
He offered another cigarette,
I said, "Yeah, for the way." I regret,
And watched him disappear
Into his wild and smoky atmosphere.

Rivers
by Erica Foster

Rioting waves make the world worse,
washing away the innocence.
Intentions are pure, right?
Imagine a world where trees have loose limbs and
Vertical roots stretching into worlds unknown,
Entrenched in the rotting wood and failing weeds, contrasting
with the coughing lungs of the forests which the rivers run
through, rioting waves trying to cleanse the land.
Silver light masks the streams in darkness.
Rivers are like veins to the heart of nature.

SEEDS
BY ERICA FOSTER

Growth and creation
Manifestation into a new creation
Determined by nature;
A strong, sturdy tree
Or a rose with thorns
Or food to fill hundreds of stomachs
With pumpkin pie

SIGN OF NATURE
BY SHANNON OLIVER

A
Tree
Forming
Branches that
Stretch on for miles
Keeping me sheltered
From the pouring rain that
Continues to fall, to my irritation
N
E
V
E
R
Ending, even in the breeze.

Soul Sisters
by Abby Coombes

Roadside, life fading away
One hundred more, shattered today

In denial, it can't be true
Why not me, why is it you?

Yin and Yang, we had a plan,
to journey life, we just began

Drives in my car, girl talk
Out with the dogs, we go for a walk

Music blasting, we sing loud and proud,
windows down, wind whipping around

A stick-and-poke Sun to match your Moon,
and the promise made to see each other soon

Bellies ache, tears stream,
infectious laughter and a joyous scream

My sixth sense, I felt you leave,
you came to me, I didn't want to believe

As opposite as night and day,
light and dark, you always knew what to say

Now people don't know the right words,
to console and express what they've heard

"One of a kind!", I want to shout
to tell them all, without a doubt

Never one to bear a grudge
Unapologetically you, you didn't judge

One in a million, my best friend,
My soul sister till the end

A void filled with longing, now I'm left empty, lost and alone
Stood on the verge waiting to finish our journey on my own.

Stand Out of My Light
by Megan Goff

Agata spent most of his days stalking the marketplace in Athens. His father would give him a small handful of coins to keep him entertained and fed and send him on his way with the understanding he would not return until the evening. Agata didn't mind terribly, his father was rather boring company and much more entertaining people populated the marketplace.

Diogenes was a frequent source of entertainment, and his unusual lifestyle attracted many visitors much to the man's dismay. One afternoon Agata was especially bored, after an altercation with his father he had been denied his usual coins and thus was unable to buy himself lunch. He had sat himself down in his usual spot, the very middle of the marketplace where he could watch the people walk past. There had been a sudden commotion and a league of fully suited soldiers stormed into the square pushing and shoving people to make room for the large chariot pulled by two regal horses. The chariot slowed to a stop in front of Diogenes where he sat in his pithos. Standing proudly at the helm of the chariot was none other than Alexander the Great. Though this didn't seem to be as impressive to Diogenes as it had been to Agata, who stood awestruck and neglected to listen to most of their conversation, more focused on the shiny metal of his breastplate and the vibrant colours of his robes, colours Agata had only ever seen in flowers and fruit. Finally concentrating again in time to hear the madman shrug off the emperor.

"Stand out of my light." He waved his hand dismissively to their ruler. Diogenes was still hunched over on the floor wearing dirty robes that may have once been white but were now a watery shade of grey.

Agata held his breath expecting to witness the man be dragged off for execution. Instead, Alexander the Great simply hummed in response, his mouth pressed into a thin line clearly suppressing a secret amusement and re-mounted his chariot to leave.

From what Agata had witnessed, Diogenes seemed immune to criticism by the highest social and political powers, whether they found him too entertaining to punish or simply respected his intellect and commitment. A frequent visitor, despite his so-called hatred for Diogenes, was an upper-class thinker named Plato. Agata had heard his name mentioned across the marketplace, a close student of Socrates, his mind was greatly respected though he himself was not too well-liked.

Agata enjoyed eavesdropping on their conversations more than most others in Athens. Their personalities clashed so severely it was always entertaining, their dynamic a far less civil mirror to that of Plato and his student Aristotle who had their disagreements but were too boring to pique the interest of Agata.

Plato and Diogenes clashed in a much more glorious way. Such as today's topic of conversation: the meaning of life. Plato had strolled through the square, following a complicated route towards Diogenes, obviously designed to make their collision appear accidental. As he approached the pithos, he stared down his nose at Diogenes who didn't spare him a glance.

"You waste your life in squalor, ambitionless. You have a mind meant for wisdom and instead, you leave it to rot." Plato had stopped bothering with niceties as Diogenes had never even made an attempt at it. He stared off into the distance as he spoke, though every passer-by knew who he was aiming his words towards.

"You waste your life preaching nonsense that normal people do not care about. It makes you unlikeable." Diogenes dismissed him with a wave of his hand still not looking up at him.

Agata's favourite thing about these two men and their interactions is their inability to turn down a fight. Diogenes may act disinterested but his deep contempt for Plato kept him involved in the eternal

"Your constant dismissal of life and its meaning leaves you stagnant. You ignore the universe as it reaches out to you, the obvious signs of what else our souls are capable of leave yours malnourished."

Plato goes on to talk at length once again about his theories on souls. He believes our souls to be immortal and that they lived before our bodies in another realm, the Realm of Forms, familiarising itself with the most basic forms of all things in the universe. He was fascinated by the way humans could recognise different forms of a thing as the same concept, different dog breeds no matter the size or colour were all categorised as dogs, and chairs no matter the material or level of decoration were all categorised as chairs. Agata had to admit it was a compelling theory to him, he has no memory of learning these categories, the exact criteria that make a dog a dog and not a goat or cow. He has no memory of learning concepts such as family, democracy, and the difference between a puddle and a lake, or a stool and a throne. Plato believes our souls ultimately yearn to return to the Realm of Forms and it is our purpose in this life to absorb as much knowledge in this mortal realm as it could manage. He felt Diogenes was wasting his short time in this life and his soul would later begrudge him for it.

"Here you go again, this nonsense. What proof do you have of this realm? Why waste your life pursuing what might be needed after death? I am perfectly content living a natural life as Man did before intellectualism and greed stole his freedom. Live for the simple pleasure, natural pleasures provided by our surroundings, eat the fruit of the tree, don't stare at it contemplating its origin as it rots away in your hand." Diogenes took a less grandiose approach to life, more grounded in the everyday needs of man. He rejected society, refused the labours of any career and the pressures of societal norms. He despised the ways money and fame could corrupt a person. Agata observed the people in his life and found evidence of this claim. His father had a decent amount of money but was focused on nothing other than making more of it. His mother was repressed by her lack of choice. After their marriage, his father moved them away from the small village of their childhoods to Athens where there was better work, after giving up her friends, her parents, and sisters to make him happy she was left with very little. Greed had taken his father as social norms had his mother. Agata yearned deeply for the life of early Man as Diogenes often described to those who questioned his choice to live in the ceramic rice jar.

After witnessing many arguments between these two men and many others, after observing everyone in this square go about their lives almost every day for years, Agata developed his own theories about life.

Plato's theory lacks emotion. His hurry to return to his Realm of Forms is robbing him of the wonders of the world, his constant need to be learning, and his belief that wisdom is above all else in this realm keeps him too preoccupied to appreciate the simpler things. He never stops to look at the sky at night, to hear the wind in the trees or watch the stray dog chase its own tail for an hour. He never slows down.

Diogenes' theory lacks beauty. It does not consider the unexplainable functions of the universe, or how our environment is perfectly assembled to sustain us. He too does not stop to appreciate the beauty, only the function of our land. His rejection of society leaves him isolated, unable to witness humanity and the benefits of human connection. As appealing as the lack of greed and repression is to Agata it would not be worth the sacrifice of humanity. He had watched Diogenes reject any attempt made by others to reach him, and the way that rejection fuelled society to keep reaching out till even the emperor came to see him. He saw their instinct to bring Diogenes back to the collective, to not leave him to his own self-inflicted loneliness.

Agata knows that beyond the stiffness and conflict of Society was the human condition. The need to love and be loved ultimately fuelled us all to argue over the meaning of life. To question the origin of our species and others. He has decided the only real purpose of living is other

people. If he were to focus on pursuing the unattainable, he would forget to stop and smell the flowers. Plato with his wisdom, Diogenes with his natural way of life, his father with his money. None of them will ever find enough, they will never be truly happy. Happiness is much more humble.

Statue of Life
by Emily Nunan

My cracks begin to crumble.

My body isn't my own.

I'm an object. A piece of art belonging to the world, for eyes to gaze over my naked curves for all eternity.

Day and night. Light and dark. Wrong and right.

Two opposites in an ongoing war to win and claim victory, to change and create, to earn the trust of one singular creation. Earth. My prison. My home.

The battle for love continuously travelling around the orbit of life. Night and day.

A raging star born to be hated for the heat it brings, its passion to burn the brightest, up against an icy asteroid born to shine in the darkest of nights with a glow so white it could blind. The sun and moon endlessly compete for the worship of all living creations.

I am confined to the warm soil which hardens around my feet. I have no escape. The heat of the fiery sun scorches my grey skin, drying me to the point of no repair, all of my fractures and imperfections illuminated and on show. The blazing star soars over me in a passionate frenzy, searching for new life to burn, forever haunting me. I was cursed. The temptation of living was taken away from me, my only purpose in life to stand tall and look heavenly for sightseers. Sight, what a funny thing, to be able to observe and watch without any notice from any living thing. I'm frozen, captured and tamed by rock and clay. A statue. Locked in time.

My eyes wander outside the garden but never away from it.

I'm tied to the dirt to watch stragglers whip past me, to take a crumb of my sorrow along with them. No voice, no way of living, just watching. I wish on a lucky star, begging to have a new beginning. A life of my own, to be freed from this garden. The garden that started it all. The beginning of time. The making of life. But I have my purpose, to watch, to witness human life form and evolve, to mend and break, to hurt and change. I am infinite.

I am life and I will continue to live as a statue frozen in time, watching you become the history of life.

The Flesh
by Carlie Wells

Flesh upon flesh,
Pressed together.
An inch feels a mile
As a kiss is sealed with a smile.

Dancing to our own rhythm,
A dance only we know,
Yet it is as old as time.
Stay in that moment, a constant rewind.

The dark gives way to light,
As the beat vibrates within the body.
A promised whisper of forever
With our next endeavour.

A smile wide with teeth
Disarms my defences,
For no walls could keep you out.
Of that there is no doubt.

THE FLOWER LOUNGE
BY EMILY NUNAN

The flowers begin their lives growing out of the lounge floor, spreading feet into soil.

Life and nature sprouting into harmony, living alongside each other as one. A union.

Rose is a prickly one, with her thorny attitude and stubborn armour. However she is a passionate soul, she holds many in her heart, her love so deep it could cut.

Bluebell is a different story, always crying with their clear liquid crystals. When a single drop falls it fills them back up to repeat the never ending cycle of weeping.

Tulip's sassy smile and two faced personality makes all cry, especially Bluebell. But she's never alone, her sisters surround her and their venomous laughter spreads.

Lily's open and aware of her beauty but can be struck as a dumb bloomer. Sometimes too stunned at how elegant she is when presenting herself to others.

Orchid stands alone and excels in being independent, never seeking help. His free spirit and wild nature allows him to hold on to his headstrong roots.

Sunflower aims high and reaches to touch the blue sky, their smile always beaming. Their happiness spreads with the buzzing bees, who feed them with their honey like pollen.

Daffodil springs out into the season singing a song with his trumpet beak, loud and strong. All his siblings follow his lead, singing and singing until they fill into the air with a lullaby.

Dandelion blooms into a bright yellow weed, surrounded by bunches of beautiful flowers. But her only wish is to be seen, to be heard, so she flies and soars high into the sky.

The flowers flourish into their own unique forms of growth, becoming wiser and smarter to share their knowledge with the little seeds, who are ready to start again within the lounge.

The Garden
by Martin Ansell

I laid all the dreams I had at your feet,
So that our walk could be safer than life.
Your heart was an Apple, tempting and sweet,
A place shimmering in beautiful light.

We danced on a daisy as big as the moon,
Naked and bare to a world we knew not.
Our garden around us: joyous with bloom,
T'was born from a time that we had forgot.

Drunk on your wine yet no stumbling step,
Nor falling nor cawing nor losing of grip.
Ahh to your side I will always have leapt,
But you desired to have my spring clipped.

> You walk away and I chase thee no more,
> I dream no longer - yet asleep evermore.

THE MIGHTY SORROW POEM
BY MYA IP

The mighty sorrow sang
One beat, two beats, three
For the world stopped; like it was
the taste of that first cup of tea
The rhythm danced upon my skin
Hands intertwined: forever to spin
Every destination, every hum, every song
One beat, two beats, three
The world clapped and danced,
Laughed and pranced
It knew never of despair, only of love and care
Taking the feet to great new highs
This sort of frolic was a must to share
So off we go – humming and spinning
To wake for a new day tomorrow
Always in favour of the mighty sorrow

THIS IS WHERE THE HOME IS
BY SHANNON OLIVER

The tree reaches out its hand, branches spreading wide,
Jutting out of the bark to carry unique leaves.
Upon these branches rest objects of all shapes and colours,
While providing a nest for those weary wings.

The tree provides sanctuary, a place to stay,
A haven for animals to sleep and birds to sing.
They call out in a melody, a delight to ears,
Before they pick up the pace and travel far away.

The tree welcomes all, turning none away.
Sheltering strangers through sun and storm.
The dampness of the rain, the blistering of the sun.
This is where the home is, if only you look closely.

The tree gifts you with shadows and provides you with all.
It asks for nothing; it stands strong on its own.
It needs nothing that humanity can offer,
For nature takes care of its own kind.

The tree wears its crown and stands tall on its throne,
Creating an image of a king, defending his subject's freedom
As a trained soldier fights to reclaim their land,
Creating an environment free from vice and pain.

The tree stays anchored to the ground by its draining roots,
Creating a strong foundation for its subjects to gloat.
Providing stability and kindness in abundance for everyone
To protect its community, for this is where the Home is.

Unrequited Love
by Emmy Johansson

"I love you" from you
Always felt too heavy
Too big and too shallow
Too much to carry

"I love you" from you
Made me feel nothing at all
Even when I tried
I guess I lied

You wanted a love
I couldn't give
You imagined a life
I couldn't live

Your arms made a cage
That shackled my body to yours
Your love was a prison
Something I had to endure

I wanted to run
Far away from you
I wanted to be free
Free of you

"I love you" from you
Made my stomach sink
It drove me mad
It made me sick

"I love you" from you
Was the wrong kind of love
It weighed me down
It made me drown

I wanted love
But not from you
I had love to give
But not to you

I wish it was different
But nothing will change
I never said "I love you"
But you thought my silence was the same

WHAT CAN I SAY?
BY HOLLY-MAY BROADLEY-DARBY

Is there much that I can say?
To change your mind,
to change your way?

Is there any words that I can speak?
For you to see our world,
for you to find your peak?

Is there anything left to show?
To give the future a chance,
to let it shine and glow?

Is there much that I can say?
Won't you take a look around,
won't you change your way?

GROWTH

bloom | flourish | mature

growth (noun)

1. *the process in people, animals or plant of growing physically, mentally or emotionally*

2. *an increase in the size, amount or degree of something*

An Ode to Tanya
by Nick George

A simple thing,
my Mat,
a safe spot
away from demands, stresses and thoughts.
On my Mat
effortless effort sparks release
igniting an inner-flame
building heat, strength and self-belief
surging, energised and alert,
yet with calm inner-peace;
lightness floods as freedom dissolves tension
allowing space for growth and extension
to observe, respect and connect
trusting deep, innate intuition.
Embracing my Mat
brings peace and tranquillity,
restorative nourishment hatched from faith and humility.
My Mat is not just a mat
but a private sanctuary
to cherish breath and b r e a t h e…
Om shanti

Becoming
by Antoni Bignell-Bird

Once upon a time, people like me were told to go underground. Cut away from those we know, change our names in secret and transition as quickly and quietly as we could.

I think that some people believe our growth still occurs like this, that I can go home on Friday and come back to work the following Monday with a full beard and flat chest. I think that they assume it's as easy as cutting a bloom from a cactus simply for aesthetic's sake.

In all honesty, some days I wish they were right. I wish I could have come out at nineteen, and handed over the seed of possibility to my GP for them to help me nurture it with hormones and cut away dead leaves. I wish I could have bloomed in time for each new job I have ever had to take, to save me from having to come out again and again and again.

I wish that process could have taken a single season like it is expected to. Instead, I kept myself in a freezer drawer, in a forced hibernation, for seven years. Then, when I finally braved the thaw, ready to grow, I was denied water for another five years. I stayed in my soil, watching the sun rise and set and the plants around me grow in ways I could not. Some got their water by paying for it. Others had waited, too. Some, the bravest, most desperate, and my most revered, turned to black market water. Others died. After my five years were up, and I was finally acknowledged by the system that should have watered me years ago, I thought that would be it.

Instead, the questions came. I lied and lied and lied. Because I knew that the truth of me, my complexity, my identity, would not fit into the box that they wanted me to grow into. And then I waited. And waited. Finally, a day after my birthday, five years, three months and six days after I knew I was ready for water, I was given it.

I think it's in our nature to be obsessed with appearance and take it at face value. We love dandelion clocks as children, as symbols of wishes yet to be made, and we pick the pretty yellow flowers and give them to our mothers as a bouquet. But then we get older, and are taught to drown them in herbicides and never, ever make a wish or else we will spread their seeds into someone's garden. And brambles, by far I think, prove my point even better. We love blackberries. We love picking them, eating them, admiring their presence at the end of summer as we ramble, knowing which ones are ripe just by looking. But the plant that they grow on? It's sharp, and its growth is unruly when left to its own device. Gardeners curse it when it grows somewhere it shouldn't, and it can turn a woodland into an impassable forest of thorns, putting an end to adventure for fear of gouged skin.

Essentially, we appreciate things only when they have a purpose for us. I, and my outward appearance, serve no purpose but to myself unless I decide otherwise. My hair has grown long, and I struggle to wear a binder so my chest doesn't lie flat. My appearance does not make identifying what pronouns I use easy for those who do not ask. Even when I am asked, or I wear a pronoun pin, it's forgotten or ignored. It feels like it's my fault for not bothering, for not conforming to gender roles, but if I had been born with the right mix of hormones and genitalia and presented my appearance the same way I do now, people would have no issue. I am not being seen as in a state of growth, I am being seen through what I lack. I am the brambles that have just finished blooming, with little green nodules growing from me, so I am still nothing more than a wild plant that gets in the way. I am a bare dandelion clock, my wishes already made and landed, but instead of being seen as the bloom of life, those seeds are a weed in a world obsessed with a status quo I want no part of. I do not make others' lives easier. I do not give them fruit that is easy to eat. I ruin their preconceptions of what it is to be a man or a woman, and I make them uncomfortable because of it.

The reality of my growth is that I am still partially underground. My first leaves, the traits that would make me easier to identify, even to the layperson, have not emerged yet. When I do tell people what I am, they are still less likely to accept it, because the big and obvious things haven't happened yet. This stagnated growth, through no fault of my own, is seen as an unwillingness on my behalf to commit. I can see it all, though. I see each and every stage and I meet it with such joy.

I am growing, I am changing. I have nearly died and rotted into a shell of a possibility so many times over the years, but I am finally, finally, becoming. I do not forget those who have died alongside me, and I mourn for them, but I remember them for who they are. That is something that will never stop. There are birds, bugs, and parasites that want me, like the others, to disappear. There are misinformed people who want to tear me from my soil, dry me out and kill me because they think I am a weed.

Maybe I am a weed, in their world. They hate that my presence disrupts their illusion of control, their belief that they can choose which plants grow where and that nature bows to their whim only. Good. They can pave us over with concrete and laws and slander, but nature always finds a way. The weeds will always win.

Breathe
by Chloe McBeath

Stinging inhales of crippling tomorrows,
Debilitating and persistent.
Consumed by the ghosts of numbed memories,
My light flickers.

Crackling exhales of darkened hope
For those 'better days'.
The reflection of brittle life, with mirrored doubt
Block me from a full existence.

The innocent years of ignorant bliss
And unknown time,
Shift to fears of wasted mortality.
When will the agony end?
Inhale… Exhale.

Dare to Dream
by Nick George

So small, this fledgling amidst family strife,
Well nurtured, much loved, yet left and bereft.
Head down, unworthy, scorned ambitions for life.
Still young, both her parents had flown the nest.

With gumption, graft, an Acharya to guide
And nourish that weak bird, her wings unfurled.
Her head held high, learning how not to hide.
She flew and flourished in a thrilling world.

Her own offspring were dared to follow dreams,
Fed hope, belief and ambition they bloomed,
Grew strong, grew up; growing away it seems.
Her fine, extraordinary life, deemed doomed.

    Now just fine, extra ordinary, blue.
    Inspired, she aspired to dare to dream too.

Free Fall
by Carlie Wells

Grains of sand upon a white beach,
Revelling in the glorious heat.
Summer times, holiday vibes.
Dancing to your own drumbeat,
Or relaxing in unstoppable tides.

Sometimes I am summer.

The beauty of a fond farewell,
The crunch of frost beneath your feet.
The brokenness of a squirrel's nutshell.
Old falling away. Bittersweet.

Sometimes I am autumn.

Harsh and unrelenting,
Icy rain, pelting hail.
Frustrated voices, augmenting.
Watching your breath, with every inhale.

Sometimes I am winter.

Freshly sown roots,
Delicate petals.
Succulent fruits,
Emerging freckles.

Sometimes I am spring.

Sometimes I am all at once,
Or simply none at all.
There are no designated months,
But rather a glorious free fall.

GROWTH
BY GEORGIA JERREY

They say we all grow differently
That I didn't want to believe
I was supposed to achieve
But you told me no
Only two months to go
And the world became blurry around me.

I'd been working on myself
To be the better person
To fight those demons
Doing the right thing
To finally be happy.

But you believed in me
Kept me going
When all I saw was darkness
You see the best of me
The light that keeps glowing
As I keep growing.

As I'm finally happy
The world is brighter
Life is lighter
I'm finally free to be me.

Hexapus
by Daphne van Hoolwerff

The goldfish in the fishbowl was fake. I wondered how I'd never noticed it before, but now all I could do was watch its glassy, lifeless eyes as it circled round, slowly sliding along the glass.

"Rianne?"

Evelien's voice broke my hypnotic stare and snapped my focus back to the office. The perpetually half-closed blinds made the room extra shady, the tall stately plants drooping slightly. From behind her desk, Evelien's green eyes stared at me intently but sternly, though she tried to smile affably. Her black hair was combed back in a tight ponytail. From this distance I could see that her foundation was breaking a bit in places.

"Yes," I said, forcing my face into an expression I hoped looked attentive and poised.

I felt my fingers tightening on the back of the chair, the metal cool and hard under my skin.

"How do you think it's going?"

My stomach tightened at the question.

"Uhm, okay, I think?"

She sighed, and in that sigh I could already hear everything that she was going to say, the words gathering in her throat and hanging over us in the air. I braced myself. My eyes flicked back to the plastic fish for a brief second, wishing I could go back to my faint amusement of a moment ago, but I found no comfort there. It was just in the middle of its trillionth circle. There was no escaping this.

A few hours later, I walked down the marble stairs, my thick soles producing a reverberating thud with every step, right into the bustle of the Amsterdam food halls. A soft cacophony of voices echoed between the walls, adding to my mind echoing Evelien's words back to me. *We just expected a bit more from someone your age.* As I stepped outside, I was met with a light drizzle. I put up my hood and stuffed my long, sleek hair under it as well as I could. I tried to keep my face hidden as I greeted the tram driver and then sat down. Huddled away in my hoodie, I hoped no one could see the tears on my cheeks, making small splashy stains on the collar of my green jacket.

As I opened the door to my dim hallway, I instinctively started kicking away the letters and folders sprawled out on my doormat. Amongst the stark whiteness of the envelopes and the chaotic colours of fast-food chain slogans, something stood out. A picture of a piece of blue, stretched out sea, contrasted by a rocky shore. A postcard? Who would... as I picked it up and flipped it, I got an inkling. *Dear Rianne, hope you're doing well. I've just returned to Agios Nikolaos for the summer as the diving centre is open for business again. Your mum said you could use a break, so I thought I'd invite you over. Plenty of space here! Let me know. Your Aunt Gemma*

With the worries of the afternoon still fresh on my mind, I flicked the card aside. I had no time to think about this now. I walked into my silent apartment and into my bedroom, the curtains still closed. I quickly kicked off my pair of skinny jeans and grabbed a pair of trackies off the pile of clothing on my chair and was out of the door again soon. I didn't pay much attention to traffic as I cycled past the roundabout, took a left and whizzed past the rows of monotonous townhouses on a long street.

So they're giving you a month's notice?" my mother said half an hour later, as I sat on her couch, a steaming cup of licoricey tea in my hand and the TV on a low murmur.

An evening talk show with some familiar faces sitting around a table, talking animatedly about a subject that I missed.

"Yes," I mumbled. "Because I haven't worked there for two years yet. Just when I thought I had some stability…"

I could see the compassion on her face and I felt myself cringe. Some strands of grey were visible amongst her pepper-and-salt coloured, chin length hair, hanging wispily around her head. I remembered when it was the same dark blonde colour as mine. She sat in the corner of the couch by the reading lamp, wrapped up in her white bathrobe and her mug of Ovomaltine in her hands. Sometimes when I looked at her, it really struck me, she was getting older.

"Well, maybe this could be a new beginning. Maybe it's time you finally started looking for a proper job."

I'm trying not to roll my eyes like I'm a teenager.

"You're twenty-nine, you have a master's degree… you can do better than these customer service jobs and the likes."

I tried to keep the defensiveness out of my tone.

"I have tried. I mean, I guess there's no harm to keep trying but… they always say they're looking for someone with different experience."

I stared forlornly into my teacup, as if trying to find the answers there. Then a question escaped my lips I wasn't sure I had fully intended asking.

"Mom, am I a disappointment?"

"Oh, of course not! Now why would you ask that?"

But I felt suspicious of this answer. She'd replied too quickly for my liking.

"You know why," I said flatly.

"Please don't keep putting yourself down for that. You have a learning disability, so what? Lots of people have lots of things."

I swirled the half-brown tea water around, the cup growing lukewarm in my hand.

"I don't know, sometimes... I feel like I can't keep up with the rest of the world. Like I'm trying to, but... I'm always behind, I can't get along, like I wasn't equipped to participate in this society..."

My mom put her empty cup of Ovomaltine down on the coffee table with a loud thud.

"Oh, shush it. It may take you a bit longer, but that doesn't mean you're incapable. You know what might do you some good? A holiday."

"But I don't have m..." I frowned at her as I put two and two together. "You spoke to Aunt Gemma?"

I stared at the TV, where some newly joined people were talking about a seemingly different subject now.

"I swear fifty percent of Dutch TV is just pointless talking."

"Tell me about it," my mom agreed. She looked at me. "Just go. Enjoy your life a bit."

I sighed. I still couldn't believe I was actually doing this as I found myself lugging my small suitcase through the landing of a TUI plane a month later, in June. It was already full of people and filled with murmur, shuffling of suitcases and the thud of the overhead lockers closing. Four hours crawled by. When I finally got off, the airport in Heraklion looked more barren and cramped than I'd expected. Signs with both English and Greek guided the way and I was immediately fascinated by the unfamiliar scribblings of the latter. Stepping out onto the brightly sunny pavement, the heat immediately slapped me right in the face. Tourist buses were lined up, people with signs of travel companies standing around, eagerly on the lookout for their customers. Rocky mountains loomed in the distance all around the airport. It was all slightly disorienting.

Yet there was Aunt Gemma waving at me, her perpetually perfectly straight bun on top of her head, not a trace of sweat or discomfort on her face. We drove through the driest landscape I had ever seen, swirly roads past parched mountains and a curious amount of decayed houses with barred windows and collapsed roofs. It looked like no one had lived in them for decades.

"I'm very sorry about your job, darling, but there's no use in moping around," Aunt Gemma said next to me, sternly keeping an eye on the road through sunglasses. "It's good that you came. It's still very quiet at the diving centre this time of year, so you can really take your time to…"

I let her babble on as I took in the environment.

"We'll see," I mumbled.

Aunt Gemma lived in a detached house high up in a mountainous area, which looked like a villa to me. The roof terrace had a wide view with nothing notable close by but an old graveyard. A few recliners stood scattered around a pool of about seven metres long and five metres wide.

I often walked out to a little beach right by a seaside café called Achinos, rocky shores on one side and tiny supermarkets, tourist shops and cafés on the other. You could rent recliners for eight euros all day and lie there with the waves rolling at your feet, the view of the sea and the mountains like an endless moving painting. I watched the other tourists from my recliner, my head under the parasol. People playing with bats, little kids running around with various tiny sea animals in their hands that they had scooped up from the water. A small sea-star, a miniature squid no larger than two knuckles of a finger. I watched the Greek locals having dinner with their family, seemingly stretching out their table time for as long as they could as they took their time with drinks and desserts.

Something that stood out to me from all these families, is that the children always seemed happy. All of them were bubbling with liveliness and playfulness as they interacted with the others on the table, kids and adults alike, and it filled me with a feeling that was warm and fuzzy but also had a slight pang at the heart of it. I wondered what it was like in their place. Their world, a safe bubble, a life stretched ahead of them that still had every possibility. Would I have been different having grown up in this warmer climate, living a more outdoorsy life by a sea that's not murky but instead held tiny wonders, safely sustained by a big circle of family and friends? Would I have been more confident, would I have lived in the moment more?

At the same time, I found there was a joy in watching and looking from the outside. Maybe I didn't always have to be participating in the world. Maybe sometimes it was enough to just observe, to bear witness.

Most mornings I just stayed by the pool in Aunt Gemma's terrace, a sun cream-stained backpack next to me with a book, sun cream and my phone. On my second last day, I was caught up in a thriller, I heard the glass doors slide open.

"Still hiding here by yourself?" Aunt Gemma said as she strolled onto the terrace, not a hair on her perfect bun out of place.

"Yep."

She shook up one of the pillows on the recliners by the water.

"Wouldn't you like to try diving some time during your stay?"

"Uhm, I hadn't really given it any more thought," I could honestly say.

"Come on darling. I'll book you a beginner's session tomorrow at ten. You don't need to have any experience, it'll be nice and easy, just bring a towel."

She walked back inside through the doors and started dialling a number on her phone.

"Yes, hi, I'm calling to see if-"

I tried not to look ungrateful. I'm not a teenager.

The next morning I made my way over with a towel stuffed in my backpack, bikini already on, and arrived at the diving centre at a quarter to ten. It looked a lot smaller than I imagined. A modest building next to the sea, like a canoeing place without canoes. A table stood outside by the window with a group of people lounging around drinking coffee, some of them with wetsuits pulled halfway down. Aunt Gemma was seated on one end next to a bulky man excitedly showing his underwater camera. By the water, two guys of which I can only assume are employees are arguing. One of them, a skinny bloke with messy dark hair, was going on a tirade to the other in French. I took up a small chat with two Germans on the other side of the table, a man in his forties and an older woman. I silently wondered about their relationship. The woman told me a bit about how she was afraid of diving too at first, but now loved it.

"You must try," she said, as they got up to join the boat that would take them to the diving site.

"And remember, this is wet in the water," the man said to me with a huge grin, clearly font of his own joke.

"First time?"

I noticed the French guy had walked up to me. His voice was a bit crackly, but in a pleasant way. I nodded.

"Don't worry, I'll hold your hand the entire time, it will just be you and me.... I'm Jeremy by the way. I'll be your instructor today."

He led me inside the small office, which had a desk, a computer and a wide range of diving equipment, and a rack full of wetsuits. He looked and sounded so chipper, not at all embarrassed about announcing we'd be holding hands soon, even though we were complete strangers. As he explained the basic diving techniques sitting in a chair opposite me, I was too focused to notice his skinny waist and legs, warm smile and bizarrely blue eyes. But I would later.

"I'm actually really nervous," I told him as he tried on a pair of goggles on me, his eyes studying my face intently.

Jeremy waved his hand dismissively.

"No worries, take it easy. Just keep breathing! That is all. I bet you that after, you'll want to go for another dive!"

Somehow his thick French accent made his enthusiasm even more infectious.

"I doubt it."

"I swear. Everyone always does."

"Okay, I want to bet", I said. "For a beer?"

The wetsuit felt heavy and stiff, and I felt wobbly as I walked towards the water slope. As I stepped into the sea and the material soaked up the water, it started to feel even heavier. I descended the slope that was laid out in awkward, unbalanced steps.

Underwater, everything was silent apart from my own breathing and swishing noises of the water as we moved our arms doing exercises. There wasn't much to look at apart from the man in front of me, his eyes an oasis of security, an anchor behind goggles. I struggled to stay on the bottom of the slope, gravity determined to keep pulling me up as if it didn't want me underwater. Jeremy clipped some extra weights on my wetsuit and steadied me. I was finally able to stay down, to be present. Then he led me further down into the water, playfully floating on his back and pulling me with him, seeming entirely in his element. I quickly got used to holding hands with a stranger. We weren't deep at all, perhaps a meter and a half, but my brain kept sending me SOS signals.

Oh God I'm underwater I can't breathe down here. Sunbeams illuminated the surface above my head, and I had an overwhelming desire to swim to it, but Jeremy kept diverting my attention back to the ground beneath us. He dug up a strange animal that looked like a hybrid between a long-legged spider and a sea-star, holding it out for me to touch, but I made a refusing gesture with my hand.

Some time and a couple of quick panicked surface visits later, he'd seemingly spotted something on the bottom again, pointing repeatedly. I could see nothing. He pointed some more. I kept staring at the sandy ground, studying it for anything out of the ordinary. Then I saw it. A small, barely visible end of an octopus tentacle stuck out from under the sand.

Jeremy's hand sunk down to meet it, giving it a small and gentle prod, coaxing it out of its hiding hole. The tentacle shifted. I looked on as Jeremy patiently continued his efforts of slowly getting the animal to come out. Then it emerged from the sand, more tentacles appearing at first, then its head too. Jeremy caught it in his hand. The octopus was small, only a bit bigger than Jeremy's hand, and seemed to have only six legs.

I was calm. The octopus's strange wobbly legs did not scare me, and I did not squirm as I reached out and touched its skin, which felt like a strange combination of rough and slimy. I'd always expected it to feel a bit like rubber, but this felt nothing like dead material. It felt very much alive. Tentatively, I let one tentacle run through the palm of my hand as I explored the squishy sensation, as if I was caressing a strand of hair. Its muscles were clearly palpable, especially as the spongy limb hooked itself lightly around my wrist. Even if its grip was loose, its strength was undeniable. Jeremy helpfully unhooked it.

Then I saw that a small cloud of black liquid was spreading through the water, spiralling around us in swirly puffs, like smoke. I questioningly looked at Jeremy. It was then that he released his grip and the animal shot off into the wide openness of the water, its six tentacles propelling it effortlessly forward as it glided through the blue. My neck strained too much to keep looking, instead turning my head back to Jeremy, who gave the octopus a little wave as he swam on in the other direction. I did the same. He laughed then, and even though it was soundless, it was a real, joyful chuckle. I smiled too.

"I wasn't sure if you'd touch it," he said softly as we came out of the water some time later, sounding genuinely surprised.

Now that we were above water again, suddenly his assured and authoritative instructor-like behaviour had evaporated. Something seemed to evaporate in me too. Before I knew it, I was sitting around the table with the other divers again, overhearing them talk about pufferfish. Jeremy strolled up to me, shoulders slightly slumped.

"So, would you like to have a drink later…?"

He said it with uncertainty and my answer came out intuitively.

"Sure, yeah."

I walked back to the hotel with my towel wrapped around me and my head in a confused state. I had the vague sensation that something had been set in motion but wasn't sure what and if it was something if it should want.

When I arrived at Achinos that night, there was some sort of big family event going on at the private terrace. A group of at least forty people all sat around long, fancily set tables, dressed in suits and evening gowns. I figured out quickly it must be a Christening. One family was even more dressed up than the rest and seemed to be the subject of an endless photoshoot, the parents proudly cradling their young son dressed in a small blazer and formal trousers. His mother was wearing a long white and silky dress. Her face betrayed she was perpetually displeased with the course of the evening, looking almost thunderous as she paced around having frustrated chats with other guests. I sat observing for a while until Jeremy was suddenly in front of me, looking somehow flustered and wearing three-quarters cargo combat trousers that made his legs look even bonier.

"Did the octopus feel threatened by us?" I asked a bit later, a small bowl of nuts, a pint of Mythos and a bottle of Stella and on the table in front of us. This was a beer choice that Jeremy had found worth mocking. "Since it was giving off that… black liquid?"

"The ink," he helpfully added.

He smiled.

"Yes, the ink!"

"Maybe we annoyed it a bit… it was a hexapus, by the way. It had only six legs."

As our conversation flowed and the twilight set in, the water aglow with the light from the setting sun, the music had changed into what sounded like traditional Greek music. Beautiful melodies spun by plucky instruments and an accordion adding an undeniably danceable, propulsive rhythm. Next to the bar, a grandma was teaching her granddaughter some dance steps. She looked like the archetypical grandmother from an old childhood story, with a grey bun and a long, wide dress that swirled around her ankles as she danced. Her granddaughter, dressed comfortably in shorts, mirrored her arm and hip movements as closely as she could, both of their bodies moving fluidly and carelessly, the joy apparent in every move they made. I was as entranced by this scene as I was by the music. Jeremy was looking at them too.

"Sometimes it's tough that everyone lives in groups except me."

I looked at him.

"What do you mean? Like everyone else has a family or is in a friend group?"

"Friend groups. When I get home in France, I don't know anyone. The ones I do know, I don't want to see. I see some old friends, maybe one, two. But everyone is in a group. I have no group."

I thought about the couple of friends I had at home. But they'd moved to different cities or started a family.

"Maybe sometimes it seems that way, that everyone else belongs and no one else is lonely," I said slowly, looking out over the water. "But that's because we're not seeing those other lonely people. Or we don't know that they are. Maybe no one really fits in a hundred per cent, but people's lives probably all look different on the inside than they seem on the outside. I mean, look at this family for example... that woman in the long white dress has clearly got some issues."

I nodded towards her. Jeremy laughed heartily and I swear it beat even the music.

"I'm just saying everything is a spectrum, you know? So, loneliness is too. And we all just sit in different places on it."

I noticed the deep direction the conversation had taken, Jeremy's face glued onto mine with an expression I couldn't quite place.

"Anyway," I said in a brighter tone. "I think it's important to look at what you do have. We're not in the worst place on the spectrum. Some people may not have a family like us... or someone to spend an evening with on a beach."

"True."

He smiled at me, but it was kind of a sad smile too. I couldn't deny the magnetic pull I felt, like I'd suddenly found myself in a strong undercurrent but was floundering, resisting, before it would carry me off to dangerous depths lurking below.

The current kept pulling as we talked more, yet my arms stayed firmly at my sides, and his stayed slumped in his lap. After having checked my phone several times and then chucking it aside, holding off the inevitable for a bit longer, it came to a point where I had to announce the hour with a dramatic sigh. It was time to go.

"Come here," he said as he stood up, and I hurried into his embrace, wrapping my arms around him.

I noticed I was smiling into his shoulder.

"Who knows, maybe I'll be back one day for our second dive."

I don't know if I believed it as I said "Yeah. Who knows."

He raised in hand in a wave.

"Bye."

It came out as a whisper. I looked at his face for as long as I could, thinking maybe I could hold onto him as long as he was still in my vision. He looked back, not breaking eye contact until he was too far away and the night engulfed him. And then he was gone. Like the octopus, like our friends, like everything else.

I wasn't ready to leave yet. I sat there for a bit, looking out over the now black water in front of me. The party behind me still showed no sign of stopping and their playlist seemed endless, the Greek instrumentals briefly interrupted by *Dance me To the End of Love* by Leonard Cohen. As I sat there absorbing everything and trying to imprint every detail of this evening into my brain, the night spun on.

The music still played and swayed in my head the next day as I stood in line with my boarding pass and passport clasped in my sweaty hands. I could see my physical surroundings, the barren walls and the shuttle bus behind the glass doors, but my mind hadn't caught up yet. As I slumped forward on the small plastic foldable table in my plane seat and closed my eyes, my hoodie pulled over me, hyper vivid visions swam before my eyes. Deep blue water and schools of coloured fish swarmed past my retina, like one of those videos they put on in a TV store to show off the picture-perfect video quality.

Even as my mum drove me home from the airport, the highway and the Dutch flat fields that I saw sliding by from the car window still somehow seemed less real to me than the beach by Achinos. It was hot here too, but it was a more humid heat that immediately put me to sleep as soon as I hit the couch. I closed the curtains.

One day kept rolling into the next. I scrolled through memes or job offers, answered emails.

THE GARDEN OF EDEN

I had tea with my mum. I was invited for a job interview in an office with eerily similar shadiness as the old one. Through the blinds, I could see shades of sun trying to penetrate the office, but never making it quite that far. Every time *Dance me to the End of Love* would show up on my iPhone's screen in my Spotify shuffle, those first few stirring notes filling my ears, I fumbled my phone hastily to press 'next'. Yet my finger never moved up to the green little heart. Jeremy's name popped up on my screen sometimes too, but that became fewer and farther between. Gemma's postcard stood propped up against a plant pot on a shelf in my living room.

Then one day in March, after having come home with wet stains on the collar of my jacket, I took it in my hands, looking at the now slightly sun faded blueness of the sea. I put it down. As I picked it up again the next day, I'd already made a decision.

This time I knew my way around the bilingual signs as I made my way through the airport. Even though the only nature around here were the stark mountains, without a drop of water in sight, I could already see and smell the sea. I stepped into the taxi, and it soon drove off into the open landscape.

Moving Forward
by Yna Lazarte

It all started with Aunt Ellen's passing.

You heard the news through your dad who messaged you while studying for your midterm exams. You cried for hours on end, listening to Aunt Ellen's favourite songs as you recalled the memories of your aunt singing along as she did the chores or played her acoustic guitar. It was as if she serenaded the whole room to life.

A week or two passed, and you attended the funeral. You greeted your uncle and his family as you made your way to the altar, where the open casket showed your aunt as she lay in peace. As you peered closer, she looked serene, as if she was asleep.

As the crowd settled to their seats, your uncle led the opening of the service with a prayer. Afterwards, the whole congregation sang in discordant harmony. You couldn't sing, as your heart couldn't bear the thought of singing praise to a higher being who had taken away your aunt.

Once the singing had ended, the congregation sat in silence as your dad, cousins, uncle and other relatives recited their eulogies. When it came to your turn, you walked toward the podium to say your final goodbyes. All you could talk about was how amazing and kind your Aunt Ellen was.

Yet, you fail to add that she was a better mother figure to you than your own mother. That, and she was an incredible sibling to your dad, especially when she supported him during a brutal divorce which involved the police, endless nights of screaming and a lengthy custody battle.

Instead, all you could do was sob uncontrollably, your dad leading you out of the podium, comforting you along with the rest of the family.

The rest of the funeral procession carried on smoothly, all the way to the burial, where the priest finally said the last rites and the pallbearers lowered Aunt Ellen six feet under.

A month after Aunt Ellen, you met Wayne.

He was in the same seminar as you when you entered your final year at university. You bonded over your love of true crime and video games, sitting on a bench in the quad of the student accommodation that you both stayed at. Just like a shooting star, you fell for his charm, wits, and his perceiving of the world through an 'obscure sense,' as he claimed.

And he liked you as well, with your sardonic smile, the way you handled yourself when you chatted to your peers, and how your eyes brightened when you passionately debated during seminars.

However, shooting stars do fall and crash down, devastating its surroundings in their wake.

You and Wayne started off constantly close to each other as the romance thrived. As time went by, his charm was replaced with arrogance, and the witty thoughts slowly became comments that belittled every word and concern you had, and that 'obscure worldview' you admired in your relationship. It turned out that he despised a certain type of people to which you belonged. The romance slowly descended to obsession and jealousy to the point that every act of forgiveness, passion and sex ended in resentment.

You had no idea who decided to end the madness you called a relationship. All you can remember is the rain pouring over your tear-streaked face as Wayne walked away from your life.

Two months passed after the heartbreak, and your wellbeing worsened. Those days, you still felt a sense of emptiness, yet you smiled and chatted to everyone with energy. You cried on the bed and begged for the pain to stop, yet you laughed away at all the jokes your friends made. You felt you were dying, yet you were breathing and alive.

It was as if the world fell apart and rebuilt itself again in an endless cycle as you stumbled through the loss and pain.

Then, one day, something clicked. Your head revealed your failures: you failed to support your Aunt Ellen when she had that diagnosis of the disease that killed her, while your dad helped her as he worked three jobs to support your studies. You even failed to be a good girlfriend when Wayne's 'friends' kept staying over for a 'project', becoming obsessed and jealous and failing to stop the arguments that occurred when he mentioned it.

You concluded that your life was meaningless and all the horrid things that happened were your own fault.

You got a knock on the door of your dorm room on the day that the incident happened.

When you opened the door, you were greeted by Lance, your childhood friend and current flatmate for the last three years.

"Hey, I'm just asking if you've done- are you okay?" His sudden change of topic threw you off as his face scrunched with worry.

"N-no I'm fine, I'm just really tired," you lied, as you gave him one of those typical 'everything-is-all-okay' grins.

"Are you sure? You look like you've been dragged around by the foot for weeks."

Truth be told, you did look like someone tied your feet together and dragged you around. Although, your wavering smile says otherwise.

"Look, I haven't had sleep for months because the diss deadline is almost up, so sue me," you reassured as Lance sighed.

" Weren't you about to ask me something?"

"Fine. I was about to ask whether you've completed Charlie's essay". "Oh, that? I already submitted it."

"Ah good, I'm just checking since you have a habit of forgetting. Anyways, I'll see you around".

Lance turned around as you gave him a 'see you, then' and he walked towards his dorm.

"Oh yeah, one more thing." He turned to face you once more as you gave him a questioning look.

"Sure, shoot."

"If you're not feeling okay, let me know."

"Will do."

After the conversation, you returned to your room silently and sat on your bed while your mind raced.

Forgetful, huh? It's better if I were left forgotten, you loudly thought. Your body automatically moved to grab your jacket while your head was on its final string holding onto whatever remained of your stable mental state.

You continued to tread along the path to your destination, toward self-destruction, as cars, transport and people go past you. It's almost as if you're non-existent.

By the time you arrived at the middle of the concrete bridge, you were about to break apart as you looked over the murky waters.

Instead, you decided to end things.

Well, you were about to end things, if it hadn't been for Lance immediately stopping you from taking that final step between life and death.

All you can recall was the screaming and sobbing, and a warm embrace before you lost consciousness.

You woke up with the scent of sterilised equipment and fresh flowers. You opened your eyes to see your dad and Lance right next to you as you lay in a hospital bed.

"That was stupid of you, doing that," Lance quietly spoke as you stared with sadness. He looked down at you with coffee-coloured eyes that shone with tears.

"Lance, please don't make this harder for her! Ame, I know you're not well, but if it wasn't for him stopping you from ju-"

"Why did you stop me?" You interrupted your dad, and Lance took a deep breath to try not to lash at you.

"Why did you decide to end your own life? Why didn't you tell me you were not okay?!" Lance's voice wavered from anger to sorrow as your dad tried to calm him down.

"Do you know why? I lost someone whose side I didn't stay beside when she passed away- someone who was a better mother to me than my own! I lost a relationship because I obsessed more over my ex's 'friendships' than what we had! I constantly blamed myself for not doing enough, so I did everyone a favour by disappearing, so nobody can worry about me at all. You have no fucking idea of how horrible it is when you try to do your best but all you do is fuck up!" You screamed as both Lance and your dad looked at you with wide shock. "All I wanted to do was to end this ceaseless feeling of being a burden to everyone so they can move on without me!" You sobbed furiously as your heart began to pour out the pent-up emotions that you held for too long. You suddenly felt both your dad and Lance hold you in a tight embrace.

"I'm so sorry Amelie, I didn't realise you felt this way for so long."

"It's okay Ame, Dad's here. We won't go anywhere, don't worry."

You were held by the two people who cared for you most as you poured out your heart through overwhelming tears.

Three months after the incident, you were assigned to a mental health advisor, who recommended you to a therapist to help with coping through the episodes and issues you've dealt with for so long.

The therapist assigned to you was friendly and allowed you to vent everything from your estranged mother to your previous relationships. The therapist would nod and write a few notes before they added insight into your moods.

By session three, you were recovering, now comfortable to

talk to your dad and Lance about your wellbeing and becoming comfortable with handling your episodes, and knowing what to do when it had gotten too much.

Months have passed, and you have passed with flying colours and graduated along with your peers.

You eventually managed to get a job as a mortgage advisor. At first, you struggled to
answer the brokers with the criteria you were trained to provide, but eventually, you got the hang of it.

You tried to impress your colleagues by talking about your life at university and the moments you had cherished, but instead your ambivalent humour, your love of everything geeky and your enthusiasm gained you a few good work friends that made the job a little more bearable.

Two years after you graduated and started your job, you met Andy.

Andy was invited by a work friend to one of your Friday night drinks sessions, and you bonded over anime references. After your friends left to go to the nearest nightclub, you and Andy instead walked towards the quiet city park. under the dark, starry sky, you talked about your jobs, perceptions of life, hobbies, and pop culture.

After a month, you and Andy got together, and you had never been with someone who treated you as well and understood you in more ways than him.

Eventually, after two years of spending time in each other's homes (more around his than yours), you two moved in together. By then you had moved on to work as a librarian, while Andy graduated and worked as an IT technician at a Fintech company.

A year later, you both were officially married.

It was a small wedding and reception, where a few family members and acquaintances were invited to witness both your and Andy's union.

The decorations and food were not too grand or fancy, but that didn't matter. The main part was celebrating a new milestone in your relationship.

Now heading to the present, you sit on your laptop, writing a draft of a story while Andy plays around with your pet shorthair cat. As you witness the poor cat trying and failing to catch a toy rat attached to a string that Andy dangles around, you think about the things that have happened and the things that someday you will face. You take a deep breath and exhale, knowing that you will have to take every day one step at a time and keep moving forward towards the future.

PACIFIC FORTUNES - A TIMELY AWAKENING
BY NICK GEORGE

Liam felt free from his old life when he received news of Tabitha's death. He'd loved her hanging on his arm, but he didn't actually love her. Their rollercoaster relationship was toxic and he knew that one way or another it would end. Liam's lips curled into a smile on reading the news alert 'Female tourist drowns in suspicious circumstances'.

Noone knew the truth and his secret was like a superpower. Feeling liberated, it was time to accept his destiny.

Four days earlier...

Rich with Italian marble and fine gold leaf, The Avar Ice gleamed more lustrously than the sun-kissed rolling waves she sliced through as she journeyed south-east in the Pacific Ocean. With Captain Fergus Jackson at the helm, the seventy-five metre megayacht carried a twenty-strong obsequious crew pandering to every need of twelve pompous passengers.

Making money was an addiction for Liam. Despite being five days into the island-hopping voyage, he had spent the morning checking portfolios and fine-tuning key client investments, much to the irritation of his long-limbed, short-tempered fiancée.

Tabitha was happy to spend his money, but intolerant of the hours he had spent building Solid Futures from a start-up. Her irksome complaints hung in the air, ignored, as a familiar pop and effervescent eruption lured him to the deck for lunch.

Strutting through the yacht's epicentre - an opulent circular dining room - he passed an antique grandfather clock displaying the wrong time, its pendulum at odds with the waves.

Ruthless ambition had resulted in Solid Futures' rapid growth, and five of its most successful hedgers were aboard the oligarch-owned yacht with their partners. The trip had been gifted by one of Liam's dubious clients as a gesture of gratitude for the returns he had reaped while hiding in the shadows.

Rock music played and the group was already in full party-mode, lauding Liam as he jumped up onto one of the ornate Quartz pedestals surrounding the Jacuzzi at the aft. Looking down on them, he revelled in their glory before raising his crystal-cut flute, and raising his voice above the Pink Floyd song that was playing.

"Ahoy, shipmates! Here's to Fiji, which I reckon we might of left a bit bruised last night!"

"To Fiji!" everyone laughed, the chaos they'd created during their frivolities ashore fresh in their minds.

"And to Tonga where we're booked in at the island's best restaurant for more fun tonight."

"To Tonga!" the friends echoed back.

"And," Liam added, looking towards Tabitha as a way of reminding her of what really mattered, "To Solid Futures!"

"To Solid Futures!"

"And to Liam Brimley!" piped up Lauren.

"To Liam Brimley!" everyone chorused, downing their Moet, so their glasses could be refilled.

Casting his glass aside, Liam clicked his fingers to signal for one of the crew to fetch him a bottle. As the chilled golden deliciousness began to lubricate the cogs of Liam's workaholic mind he finally began to relax, even allowing beautiful Tabby's nauseating twaddle to wash over him.

Lauren and Liam had worked together since their first jobs on the trading floor a decade ago. She was a well-connected Cambridge graduate from a privileged background; her close friendship with roguish Liam was considered peculiar and ill-judged by many. Yet this yin and yang was pivotal to their joint success; opposing, contrary forces balanced in precarious equilibrium. Harmonious on the edge of a precipice.

For, Solid Futures had facilitated a reckless investment placed by a rookie trader that had led to the oligarch's six-figure windfall, and his subsequent offer of the charter in gratitude. If Liam hadn't been high at the time, he would have pulled the naive speculation and sacked the rookie for incompetence. So it was that the mishap proceeded unchecked and, combined with a freak upturn in a stagnant market, inadvertently reaped a highly fruitful return. Hubristic by nature, Liam had sacked the rookie anyway, and greedily devoured the glory. By the time the luxury trip had been arranged, Liam's recollection was that his inherent ability to foresee market abnormalities had resulted in his masterminding of the lucrative deal.

With precision and expertise, Captain Jackson effortlessly docked at the Vava'u harbour and the entourage disembarked, gathering under the shade of a palm tree.

"Where are the rides?" Liam barked at one of the crew. His temples began to pulse. "Can't you get anything right?" he bellowed, punching the tree and startling a pair of geckos which scuttled up the trunk to hide in the fronds.

Four bulbous eyes watched as the posse turned their noses up at the local taxis, and set off on the twenty-minute walk along the beach. The evening sun radiated warmth as a light breeze gently wafted fine white sand along the shore. Liam's anger lifted as he regaled his friends with stories, feeding on the admiration they exuded while hanging on every word of his embellished tales. Except Lauren, who knew the truth. And Tabitha, who didn't care.

"This beach is ridiculous, my shoes will be ruined," Tabitha whinged, her feet sinking in the sand.

"I'll be your chariot, Princess," said Liam, whatever he'd taken back on the yacht, succeeding to lighten his mood.

Lauren took hold of her husband's hand, rolling her eyes, as Liam cradled Tabitha and took her back to the coastal road where a cluster of shabbily-dressed, elderly Tongan women were selling cheap jewellery and craftwork on the verge. Not appeased, Tabitha's grumbling continued.

"It's not good enough that decent transport wasn't sorted," she bleated. "And you should've told me we'd have to walk on this stupid sand and I'd have worn flats."

His impatience rising, Liam retorted "Jesus, Tabby, I haven't got a crystal ball. And if I did, I'd be checking the markets, not your fucking footwear. You can't even walk in those things, I don't know why you wear them."

"Because they're Jimmy, fucking, Choos," she said, exasperated by his ignorance.

The others had followed them to the road, and all eyes turned towards one of the peddlers who was quietly chanting. She looked frail. Strands of wiry grey hair poked out from an emerald-coloured headscarf which swathed her head and draped onto her bony shoulders. Her mantra intensified as she stooped over a cracked crock-pot as it emitted smoke. By her bare feet was a cardboard sign: Fortune Teller -100T$.

"The plume is the vessel," she croaked, coughing as the smoke thickened. "Pulotu signals mortal presence, ripe for enlightenment. Destiny can be unleashed, for I can foretell the morrow." She stopped, wheezing, to catch her breath.

"Get this for my story," Tabitha mischievously whispered into Liam's ear as she made her way to a rickety chair opposite the smouldering pot.

Liam stepped forward, placing two fifty pa'anga notes into the crone's arthritic hand. Her large, hooked nose and sagging jowls were visible, even though she remained facing downward. She spoke with rasped breath.

"The plume is the vessel and Pulotu's desire is strong."

The group watched mockingly as the crone took Tabitha's diamond-clad left hand, gently turning it and unfurling her slender, perfectly manicured fingers. Chanting faster, with intermittent gasps, she ran a calloused finger along the crease lines of the younger woman's open palm.

"This is Insta gold," said Liam, having pressed the red dot on his screen and zoomed in.

Lauren looked perturbed while the others stifled their sniggering.

"Oooo, the plume is the vessel," he mocked, looking up towards his friends. "If she can see the future, I'll take her back to Solid Futures to earn some real fucking money."

The laughter grew, but when Liam looked back at his screen he gasped. The crone's shrivelled face had twisted towards him. Partially hidden under drooping, hooded lids and almost obscured with thick, opaque cataracts, her ancient eyes were enchanting iridescent shades of green. Liam gathered himself, and continued to record, looking defiantly towards the old woman.

In a coarse whisper, she uttered "Hemoana is angry." Her glowering, mottled eyes dropped from Liam's smirking face to his phone, channelling something unseen which penetrated the lens. The phone buzzed and abruptly died.

"Shit, the battery's gone," Liam cursed.

"Well, if you can't capture it for socials, what's the point?" Tabitha huffed, tottering to stand up. Without a word to the old woman, the crowd left, thrusting their presence onto the Polynesian islands' most renowned fine dining restaurant.

The evening was filled with raucous frivolity, albeit tarnished when the sommelier presented a bottle of 2020 Guix Vermell instead of a 2018, and Tabitha rejected her filet mignon.

"I ordered rare, I can't eat this," she said, prodding the bloody slab of meat with her knife. After she created a spectacle, vociferously rejecting a second steak, a defensive chef emerged from the kitchen.

"Your steaks have been prepared and cooked to perfection," his clipped pronunciation betrayed his outward calm. "May I suggest, in future, you request your steak 'blue'?"

Equally defensive, Liam retorted "Well may I suggest, in future, you should go easy on the flambé or you'll take this place down. In fact," he shouted to the resort manager who had been alerted to the ruckus, "If we don't get that bottle of 2018 I ordered, *I'll* take this restaurant down." The wording of a slating tweet began to be composed in Liam's mind.

In the early hours they stumbled back to The Aver Ice. Liam placed his phone on the charging deck in his cabin, not noticing the virescent hairline crack on the lens.

On waking, Liam was irritated to find his phone hadn't charged. It was still dead when Captain Jackson steered away from Tonga towards Bora-Bora. It sat, lifeless, while the yacht's guests' drank cocktails and played watersports, interspersed with griping at the crew, including Liam's demand for the defective charger in his cabin to be replaced.

That evening the guests were devouring an extravagant five-course supper in the circular dining room when Captain Jackson made an announcement.

"We are currently travelling at a gentle twelve knots, due east and passing the one hundred and eightieth meridian at fifty-four degrees north, and one hundred and eighty degrees east and west. In layman's terms, we're crossing the international timeline, so please set your clocks back by twenty-four hours."

He switched off the intercom and looked starboard from the bridge. The stars shone brightly in the cloudless sky and, sitting high above the horizon, the almost-round moon glowed. A flicker of light flashed in his peripheral vision, vanishing as quickly as it had appeared. The captain rubbed his tired eyes. When he looked back up, the shimmering light had returned. Fluorescent whites and luminous greens danced down from the heavens. Captain Jackson had spent almost thirty years at sea, but had never seen aurora borealis in this region before. He briefly considered informing the guests of the phenomena but, mesmerised, slowly eased back into his chair. The glowing shafts moved slowly at first, gently caressing the night sky as they ebbed and flowed like celestial waves. The meandering phosphorescence branched out and recoiled, as if a magnetic presence was at work. Intensifying, the light beams evolved into brighter green hues, pirouetting and pulsating in the inky sky. Each undulating beam became more vibrant, oscillating until reaching a visual crescendo… before gently fading away. It was breathtakingly beautiful. Almost transcendent, thought the captain as he watched in awe. A shrouded energy hung in the ether. The captain didn't see the last viridescent glow which hovered directly above the yacht for several minutes, gaining magnitude before metamorphosing into swirls, finally spiralling down, clockwise, penetrating The Avar Ice.

The crashing waves became still. Beneath the flat surface, the dark ocean held an unearthly emptiness. The depths that had thrived with a multitude of marine life lay dormant. All the creatures had fled, and an eerie silence hung between the megayacht and the ocean bed.

Just short of an hour later, stumbling into bed, Liam was delighted to see his phone was finally fully charged.

As brunch was served in the circular dining room, Liam unlocked his phone to check the last few days' missed notifications. He stopped his thumb from scrolling as an unfamiliar double-ping and momentary green glow announced a news alert '5 dead, as fire destroys $13m Minerva Reef Resort'. Clicking onto the report he read that flames ripped through the kitchen, restaurant and bar. It was thought everyone had been evacuated, but a family had been trapped. The head chef and sommelier had returned to the flame-engulfed building to help the couple and their three young children to escape. All five perished at the scene.

"Listen to this," Liam said, reading the news story out to the others. "It's a fucking tragedy - thirteen million up in smoke!"

"Probably caused by that idiot chef burning a steak tartare," Tabby jibed, laughing at her own joke. Liam continued reading that the fire had started at around ten o'clock on Wednesday evening.

"That can't be right," he muttered, noticing the article was dated Thursday, August eighteenth.

He checked his watch, today was Wednesday, 17th. They had crossed the timeline and lost a day. That had to explain it, he concluded, struggling with the temporal logistics. But, he pondered, irrespective of the date, they hadn't left the resort until well into the early hours. Maybe the fire had started at 10 o'clock this morning? Studying the article more thoroughly and clicking on a video of an eye witness. The clip showed the resort manager by a charred Minerva Reef sign, a perfect full moon above her left shoulder. Tears rolled from her bloodshot eyes, streaking the ash on her face as they fell.

"We thought we'd got everyone out, but then we heard screaming from the suite on the top floor. Our head chef, Jasah, and sommelier, Abhi, went back in to help them out. But," she sobbed, "They didn't come back. None of them came out."

Unsettled, the facts bounced around Liam's mind and he kept dismissing a deranged, recurring thought until it hung heavy in his head and heart. Rational thoughts were weighted down making room for an absurd explanation.

"Oh my God. The fire's gonna to happen tonight," he said out loud.

"Don't be crazy," scorned Tabitha, while Lauren looked at him with concern.

Querying his own sanity, Liam looked up at the antique grandfather clock, its pendulum in constant losing battle to keep in rhythm against the rocking ocean; the precision of its exquisitely crafted, harmonic oscillation faltering in an alien world.

"Fuck it. Even a broken clock is right twice a day," Liam said as got up to find Captain Jackson.

By 9pm, the yacht had changed course and returned at top speed to the Vava'u harbour. Concerned for her friend's mental health,

Lauren ran with Liam along the beach and endeavoured to calm the antagonised resort manager as Liam rampaged the corridors screaming for everyone to get out, making his way up to the top floor where he pounded on the door of the penthouse suite. Despite Lauren's pleas, the police were called and Liam was taken to Neiafu police station where he was locked in a cell for the night. Lauren returned alone to the yacht, and committed to get Liam onto a rehab programme as soon as they arrived home.

Detective Sergeant Filipe Paea was an experienced officer. Meticulous, precise and calm, his quiet tenacity had gained him an enviable reputation throughout the Tongan Police Force. Not much escaped an interrogation by Filipe Paea.

"Did you threaten arson at Minerva Reef Resort following an altercation on the evening of Tuesday the sixteenth of August?"

"No!"

"We have several witnesses and CCTV footage claiming the contrary."

"Well, yes, I said stuff, but I meant I'd damage their reputation, not burn the place down."

"Did you return to the venue on Wednesday the seventeenth of August to carry out your threat?"

"I returned, yes. But no, it wasn't a threat, it was just banter."

"Banter? Hmmm. We have CCTV footage from 9.23pm of you alerting staff and guests about a fire that is estimated to have started at around 9.55pm. How can that be, Mr Brimley?"

"I... I... How bad was the fire? Did anyone die?"

"Was that your intention, Mr Brimley?"

Perspiration prickled Liam's forehead. "No comment," he said.

The questions were repeated until the detective sergeant concluded Liam was unlikely to provide anything more to aid the investigation, and released him on bail pending further enquiries.

As soon as Liam's personal belongings were returned, he checked his phone, swiping away market updates, looking for any news alerts. He clicked on 'Suspected arson at Minerva Reef Resort' and let out a sigh of relief on discovering there was no loss of life. He then groaned as a mugshot of his own face looked back at him, and he read that a disgruntled past-diner at the restaurant was being investigated by police. A video clip showed the man who had, thanks to Liam, escaped the penthouse suite.

"It was so terrifying," he explained, "There was a lot of commotion which woke us, but we didn't realise it was a fire until we saw smoke coming into the room. It all happened so fast. We just grabbed the children and ran. Flames were already coming up through the floor."

Mixed feelings raced around Liam's frazzled mind as he walked through the town's marketplace, slowly making his way towards the harbour. His senses felt magnified as he filled his lungs with deep breaths and looked around at people around him, living normal lives. Despite the illogical madness, he felt a clarity he had never experienced before. Everything around him seemed different, colours more saturated, senses more acute. He looked up at a flock of doves, marvelling at their bright green wings and red crowns. He smelt something fishy as he passed a row of street food stalls, smoke rising up as a young woman with braided hair partially covered by a green bandana seared chunks of marlin, wahoo and tuna above an open pit.

Euphoria that he'd saved five lives was offset by the predicament he'd got himself into. How could he defend himself with mumbo-jumbo he didn't even believe himself. Was this just a crazy, drug-induced dream? Walking up to a ylang ylang tree, he leaned against the trunk and sank down to the ground, holding his head in his hands. The woman from the seafood stall approached, crouching down to touch Liam lightly on the shoulder. As he looked up past her kind smile, he saw her dark caramel eyes had flecks of olive green in them.

She leaned close to him and whispered into his ear "Don't fight Hemoana. Embrace your destiny."

Pulling back slightly to look intently into Liam's eyes, she cupped her hands around each side of his face. Gently, she touched her nose to his before returning to the fire pit, seemingly disappearing into the smoke that rose from the coals.

"The plume is the vessel," Liam muttered under his breath before he continued his walk back to the yacht.

The others were laughing and squealing as they rode jet skis out on the ocean, except Lauren who was in the dining room listening to music. Spotting Liam, she jumped up, letting out a sigh of relief. They embraced for longer than either intended, neither wanting to let go. The Keane song Lauren was listening to merged into the swell of the waves, as Liam released her and walked out to the deck.

He looked beyond the horizon and felt a shift deep in his psyche. A lightness and sense of purpose. A serene moment of clarity, interrupted by a double-ping and momentary green glow on his phone.

Ruin - a song
by Jessica Lote

I'm standing in the middle of the open road.
I look around and do a full 360 – nothing.
No people, no birds, no sound
and no signs of life other than myself.

It is as if all life known has disappeared
and it is just me left on Earth.
Maybe I'm dreaming, maybe it is all in my head,
but if something happened here, it was a war I missed.

Tell me, am I in control?
Am I all alone in this ruin?
Help me, 'cause no one's around.
How will I survive in this ruin?

I walk. I am so alone,
there's no one out here who can see me.
This sickness has me walking a lonely road.
Now the whole world is in ruin.

Tell me, am I in control?
Am I all alone in this ruin?
Help me, 'cause no one's around.
How will I survive in this ruin?

TikTok - Life Has an Expiration
by Lasma Brauke

The tired face reflected by the unnatural light,
Time gets wasted like a teen on a Saturday night.
Full of happy faces, sexy dances, and life hacks,
Algorithms working on the consumer data tracks.

All the books unread and paintings unfinished,
Put up a green screen to feel less diminished,
There's no charger for drained inspiration,
Like, share and subscribe to the desperation.

Mountain not worth the like won't get hiked,
Food is getting cold, but the lighting isn't right.
Nothing is more important than outside validation,
Addicted to easy dopamine hits and trend rotation.

The real issues are often ignored and scrolled by too fast,
Get stuck on celebrity drama, constructed for fame to last.
Living through the lens of some stranger's aspiration,
The clock strikes midnight, no sleep for the red-eyed nation.

Spend your hours wisely, do what makes you feel good,
Just don't say sorry, if only I had the time then I would.
Oh, it's so easy to waste something that will never come back,
Start living now, don't wait for the screen to go black.
Just remember: TikTok - life has an expiration.

Tree of Life
by Shannon Oliver

They took an axe, broke it through the middle,
To see the heartwood lay in its centre,
But that tree was old and far too brittle,
So it was broken by a tormentor.

No chance of it being fixed, or repaired,
A scar to remind the stump of failure,
That beautiful trees could not be compared
To others exploitative behaviour.

I saw myself as an object, broken
For the approval of one harsh mentor,
But perhaps someone will find nature's core,
Seeing beauty through the deformed centre

> Turning scars into signs, that you can heal,
> When you see beauty inside you as real.

WISHES
BY EMMY JOHANSSON

I wish I dared to stand a little taller
Speak a little louder
Laugh a little harder

I wish I could run a little faster
Walk a little further
Dance a little freer

I wish I was a better daughter
A better sister
A better friend

I wish I was kinder
Softer
Calmer

I wish I was meaner
Tougher
Angrier

I wish I was prettier
Funnier
Smarter

I wish I could dream a little bigger
See a little clearer
Love a little deeper

I wish I was a little bolder
A little stronger
A little happier

SURVIVAL

resilience | endurance | life

survival (noun)

1. *the state of continuing to live or exist, often despite difficulty or danger*

2. *(from something) something that has continued to exist from an earlier time*

A Silent Soul
by Emily Nunan

I want to touch the moon and see the galaxy
But I am not strong enough.

The petals of this rose are falling more and more -
forcing a failure to dig deeper into me, pinning me down until I
feel empty.

I loathe the way my person speaks. The way my person feels.
What is fear? And why can I never conquer it?

This feeling eats away at me until I feel nothing -
an emotionless zombie searching for brains.

An echo at full volume, screaming at me.
No movement. Forever crying. Losing interest.

I want to speak up but I will forever be silent.
A silent girl with black venom pumping evil words into her soul.

THE ENGLISH COLLECTIVE

Beyond the Forbidden Fruit
by Nick George

Jodie

Exhausted, back aching, head pounding, Jodie refused to stop and catch her breath. She pulled a suitcase sporting a squeaky wheel and stooped under the weight of a large ruck-sack which, between them, held her entire life. She wearily trudged up the crazy-paved path to the yellow front door of the ramshackle house. Set close to north Devonshire's coastal cliffs, promising a home for the homeless.

It was a positive move, one that would help her to reset, yet Jodie hadn't fully come to terms with the disruption and damage she'd endured over the last eighteen months. Her life had become as chaotic as the sensationalist tabloid stories she had coaxed out of the naive and desperate. She realised, in hindsight, that she'd sacrificed everything for a pretty shameful career - manipulating the truth to finance a deluded existence and a wasted life.

Being a journalist had, however, furnished Jodie with an ability to adeptly read people, and she immediately warmed to Orchard Cottage's owner. Sally's welcome smile penetrated the defensive barrier Jodie had painstakingly constructed - 'a coping mechanism', her shrink had suggested, charging her two hundred quid for the privilege.

Sally's warm, brown eyes were magnified by thick-lensed, tortoise-shell framed spectacles that she repeatedly pushed up the bridge of her nose.

Jodie's case worker had explained that Sally Harris and her husband previously ran an idyllic B&B until he left, moving abroad with one of their guests. Sally's defiant response had been to close the business in favour of renting rooms to social services, insisting on providing not just a room, but a home to those who found themselves alone, floundering in an unjust society. 'Her coping mechanism?' Jodie wondered. Seemingly Sally had created good from her personal tragedy; an act of kindness that, perhaps, also soothed her older wounds. She'd had the strength to make it happen. It was this, as much as the privacy of the remote setting, that had drawn Jodie to Orchard Cottage.

"Hello, my love. You must be Jodie. I'm Sally, but you can call me Sal," beamed the stocky landlady as she bent to pick up a pile of post from the doormat and ushered Jodie inside.

The train journeys and long taxi ride had taken their toll, and Jodie gratefully accepted a seat at the rustic kitchen table while Sal bustled, placing the post to one side and setting out mismatched crockery.

"There's tea in the pot, and an apple cake's just come out the Aga, so you sit yourself down and make yourself at home."

Sal's West Country accent soothed Jodie's throbbing head, while the kitchen's cinnamony warmth radiated her skin. She soon was drinking a mug of strong, steaming tea and tucking into a generous slice of the most delicious apple cake. Her tense shoulders relaxed a little as she let the still-warm, buttery cake liquify in her mouth. The sharpness of the apples offset the sweetness, tantalising and toying with her taste buds. For the first time since closing the door on her husband, her job, and her whole world, Jodie felt safe. She silently thanked the God she had been cursing for a year and a half. This place is truly to die for.

"The Bramleys have started to ripen early this year," Sal jabbered, cutting herself a slice.

As they ate, Jodie learned about the local area and Orchard Cottage's quiet routine.

"Not many house rules; just tidy as you go, stick to the laundry rota on the notice board," Sal nodded towards the cork board next to the fridge, "And stay out of the orchard. Residents are forbidden from going near the fruit trees."

Jodie looked up at her host, temptation rising as her inner child felt a defiant urge to pick at least one apple during her stay.

"Some of the branches got weak in the storms, and we don't want you getting hurt," Sal added with a smile, shuffling about the kitchen.

She moved on to tell Jodie about the others staying at Orchard Cottage.

"You'll like Toby, a gentle giant, but a silent one - been mute since some army trauma. Been here four years and never uttered a word. Not one! He takes solace outdoors. Great help with the veggie patch, chopping wood and all that though.

"Then there's Angel," she went on, "Nice girl, but a bit messed up, bless her soul. Troubled by voices in her head and obsessed with conspiracy theories and other nonsense. And, little Dolph, bless him. Partial to a bit of the wacky-backy, calls it his medicine! But he's a good lad. Says he's moving back to Portugal soon. Shame, but needs must."

Jodie enjoyed the no holds barred introduction to her housemates but made a mental note not to reveal too much about herself to the gossiping landlady.

"Most move on within six months or so," added Sal, pushing up her glasses - more out of habit than need. "This place is a pit stop for most, but feel free to call it home for as long as you want."

After clearing up, Sal pointed out the laundry room and lounge before scooping up Jodie's suitcase and ruck-sack and, despite being well into her sixties, bounded effortlessly up two flights of stairs to Jodie's attic room. At five foot three, the low ceiling didn't bother Jodie. Simply furnished, the room's double-aspect windows rattled slightly as the north wind picked up.

Jodie unpacked and re-checked her phone. Still no signal.

She made her way back down to the lounge, where an eclectic mix of armchairs, sofas and side tables created the feel of a dentist's waiting room. At the far side of the room, wisps of smoke rose from someone sitting hunched, motionless. Between slender fingers, a cigarette smouldered, diminishing to a precarious pillar of ash. The young woman seemed lost in thought, a bullet-journal balancing on her knees as she looked, pensively, out beyond open French doors.

"You must be Angel," Jodie called out more brightly than she felt.

Closing the journal, Angel turned sullenly, giving a slow, menacing nod, her olive, feline eyes resting on Jodie.

"So, you got Casey's room, then." A statement, not a question.

Angel looked back towards an enormous man digging around some fruit bushes. The wingback armchair swallowed her petite frame making her head appear disproportionately large. Bleached hair scraped into a tight ponytail revealed auburn roots, and accentuated her prominent, freckled cheekbones. As Jodie stepped closer, she noticed scars on Angel's thin arms. The tension in the air was palpable.

"Anyone know you're here?" asked Angel, breaking the silence.

Jodie sure as hell hoped not. The directness of the strange question unsettled her - she was reluctant to discuss her delicate personal situation, yet didn't want to appear rude.

"Not particularly. I'm kind of trying to start afresh," she offered. Then, in a bid to steer the conversation away from

herself, added "So, where's Casey moved to? Are you two friends?"

Angel held her gaze on the raised beds where rambling,

prickly blackberry bushes stood alongside neat rows of tomato plants; the undisciplined and the orderly, both bearing fruit. She took a long, final drag on her cigarette and stubbed it out before turning on Jodie with a penetrating stare. Angel's expression - both damaged and damaging - made Jodie wonder if the voices Sal mentioned were at work.

Another awkward silence fell across the room.

"I dunno," Angel finally whispered, "She didn't say nothing. She just…" after pausing as if she'd glitched, Angel raised her hand, extending her fingers while making a 'poof' sound.

Sal was right, this one was messed up. Sod this. Jodie had her own shit to deal with. She wasn't in any position to get involved with Angel's paranoia, neurosis or whatever the fuck was going on.

"Yeah well, sometimes people just need to get away, do their own thing for a bit," Jodie offered before escaping to the sanctuary of the kitchen.

Jodie startled Sal, who was engrossed in the contents of an envelope she'd picked up earlier. Something briefly flitted behind Sal's eyes.

"Pwah! All this junk mail," Sal grimaced, hurling it into the kitchen bin, and then her beaming smile was back.

Angel's journal

Days clean: 178   *Anxiety: 7/10*
Calories: 948   *Depression: 6/10*

A newbie arrived today. I reckoned having someone else around might of helped, but she couldn't get away from me quick enough. She was a bit of a snooty bitch tbh, not like Casey. I could trust Casey. Praps I should of been nicer to the newb, but I ain't got time for that. I'm desperate to find out what happened to Case, and stop anyone else going AWOL. To stop me going AWOL!
Back when Crystal took off I weren't even bothered. I mean she was a right dickhead, wouldn't stop fucking talking, prattling on all the

fucking time. And I reckon it was her who robbed my bag. But it was weird how she just took off without saying nothing to no one. I reckon Toby freaked her out, always lurking around her room stalking her but never saying nothing. Sal should chuck him out, I know he helps her and stuff, but he dont even stick to the house rules. I keep thinking that maybe Toby done something to Crystal and Case found out. Then maybe he did something to Case too, so she couldn't blag. I've tried to tell Sal something ain't right, but she just asks if I've taken my meds.

That's the problem once you've been banged up on a psych ward, no one takes you seriously.

Jodie

The branches in the orchard groaned in the wind as Jodie looked out at the dark, starless sky, celestial light shrouded by low clouds. She drew both sets of curtains and climbed into bed, her exhausted body welcoming the soft mattress and fresh linen. But an unease prevented her from sleeping that first night at Orchard Cottage. After tossing and turning for several hours, she got up and crept downstairs to pour herself a glass of water.

Turning on the tap, Jodie felt an eerie shiver as her mind replayed Sal's fleeting, uncharacteristic expression earlier. Jodie had come to Devon to keep her head down, but she couldn't shake the feeling that something was amiss. Sal had seemed riveted by that junk mail.

Jodie was conscious that her ability to sniff out a story hadn't always ended well, but her investigative antennas were buzzing. Once a journo, always a journo, she reminded herself as her eyes

hovered over the bin. Flipping the lid, she prodded beneath apple peelings and scraps from the supper they'd all happily shared. But there wasn't any mail - junk or otherwise.

Toby

Sitting on wooden floorboards with his back against his bedroom door, Toby heard the creaking stairs giving away Jodie's descent to the kitchen. His fists bunched the quilt laying across him, his imprisoned mind erratically flitting between self-preservation, panic, denial and terror. Between following his instincts or fighting them. Toby's heart pounded. Be good, be good, be good. Sweat beaded on his thickset forehead and around his temples, a semi-formulated plan taking shape in his frenzied mind. He tried to fight the temptation to follow Jodie downstairs. Gripping his quilt closer, he tightly squeezed his eyes, but nothing would stop the burdened prefrontal cortex of his brain from triggering flashing images. Images of her lifeless body, like frames from a movie.

Toby hauled himself up from the floor and felt a pump of adrenaline as he pulled on the cord of his dressing gown. Feeling its strained tautness as he tightened it around his waist helped him regain a sense of control.

He took slow, lumbering strides and made his way down the stairs, carefully avoiding those that creaked.

THE ENGLISH COLLECTIVE

Bleak Beauty
BY NICK GEORGE

Cloud-shrouded iconic rock
Giant's great throne or tomb?
Enticing me into your folds
Where myths and mystery loom,
This humbling, majestic mound calls with silent echoes, striking
Scenery, woodlands and greenery breaking into dark damp stony
gloom.

Razor ridges and scooped cirques spill
From glacial battles carved
Radiating from her craggy crown
Seared with volcanic scars,
Roaring rampant water falls to flanked dark, iridescent lakes
Tarnished metallic glow within shimmering shores hugged in
valleys vast.

I awe in wonder and wander in awe
Amidst the beauty, bleak and eerie
Enduring magic hangs in the air
From tylwyth teg fair-haired fairies,

Footsteps of bygone grafters on these slopes steeped in history
Etching connection of quarries, mines and rambling ramshackle
bothies.

Whispering mists grope ancient marshes
Enigmatic boulders, slate and scree
Taking challenged breath as steep air thins
Amidst breath-taking scenery,
Eagle-eyes gawk pinnacle-cloaked peaks enshrined in lingering mist
Masking imperceptible, spectacular views looking down on reality.

Yr Wyddfa, a fickle beast, luring and inhospitable,
Glimmering warmth in the crevices of its icy desolation.

Botany
by Carmen Buckley

Wormwood, lavender, sage, rosemary.
A muddled concoction bubbles.
Sweet, fragrant, natural of this earth.
Jasmine, rose, milkweed.
Dashed into the pot.

Glass clinks together as bottles line the shelves.
Ready to be filled with that sweet, sweet brew.
Corked and labelled accordingly.

A botanist's job is done.

Fortitude
by Eli Hill

The caged lion
Roars.
Captivity cuts deep
For the former king of the savannah.
Forever destined
To observe from a distance.
A player perpetually benched,
Kept waiting in the wings.
A strange sort of death –
Mourning a life,
While trying to live another.
Life on the sidelines
An incomplete existence
To one seldom quiet,
Full of warmth and affection.
All now relegated,
Resigned,
To a life behind bars.

If the lion loses its roar –
Clips back its mane –
Is he still a lion?
His bones
Hollow,
Paper-thin skin.

Yet,
Not so delicate.
The mind of the King,
Strong.
The spirit,
Unbroken.

GOING UNDER
BY CARLIE WELLS

Sometimes it gently washes over you,
Cocooning soothingly.
Lapping at your skin –
Lovingly.
Silent, still, calm-
Peaceful.

Sometimes it's a torrent.
Crashing into your bones,
Bending limbs, Pounding skin.
It's unstoppable.
It's unrelenting.
It's unyielding.
Yanking you under as you try to stay afloat.
Never-ending.

Our Course
by Holly-May Broadley-Darby

This is our life,
this is our course.
This is where we're meant to be.

This is our life,
this is our course.
This is our destiny.

This is our life,
this is our course.
We are one big family.

This is our life,
this is our course,
and you can't change that for me.

Sad Souls
by Emmy Johansson

There is sadness
in his eyes
Even when he smiles
He tries to hide it
but I see –
And I wonder if maybe,
maybe he's just like me?

Spiralling
by Alexandra Allen-Smith

Letters, words, different shapes; struggling to find their place.
A space for each one to go; where though, I don't know.
Each line is a complete mess. It'll do, I suppose, I guess.
How will I survive?
Struggling to stay alive
Drowning in a sea of ink
No room to breathe, no room to think.
Voices whirling round and round; unable to make a single sound.
Here I lie on the floor
Looking for something; something more.
Trying to find a deeper connection
Waiting for divine intervention.
The artist is lost.
The scholar is gone.
My mind simply wanders on.

SILENT, ICY, SCREAMS
BY NICK GEORGE

Pain throbs in my temples as I regain consciousness and try to decipher where I am. Somewhere pitch black. Intensely cold. I can hear a monotonous hum, interspersed with rasping.

Realising the rasps are my parched, sporadic breaths I try to swallow, but my throat is too dry, my mouth is bound.

Gaffer tape?

Whatever it is, is depleting me of oxygen and stifling my attempted screams.

Hands bound tightly, I can't lift myself from the cold, solid floor. Confined from lashing out, I lie shivering, both from utter terror and the sub-zero temperature. Confused memories and thoughts morph in my mind, diminishing as a light - bright, yet warm - lures me, sweeping me with a sense of hope. Listening to the comforting hum of the freezer, I let go. Welcoming the light, I succumb, I let it take me. I feel a release.

The light intensifies, growing brighter as my silhouetted saviour reaches out and pulls me up. Pulls me back.

THE ANGEL INSIDE
BY HOLLY-MAY BROADLEY-DARBY

I often stare up at the sky,
wishing I could just fly.
Spreading my white feathered wings,
and making beautiful gold rings.
Dancing through the clouds,
showing off and being so proud.
With a bright dress, flowing behind,
almost making everyone blind.
Maybe an angel could grant me this,
and give me my final kiss.

THE OLD REPORTER
BY JORDAN BAND

A common sight in the little town
The man with the bags appears.
Camera bag, shopping bag, bag on back.
Camera out snapping away.

Weathered face by the winds of life
Looking down the lens at the grand opening
Of a takeaway shop, the ribbon-less, open door
Welcoming the horde of one.

Putting away the camera into one of the bags,
Ink stains from print and picture, mark the callous
Tips of the fingers soon to be typing away
In his usual place.

A ring on the finger caught in the strap,
A too-tight gold band never removed
Since the day it was put on
For it is for someone else.

Sitting at a bench, bag on back removed
Typewriter out, fingertips drifting
Over the keys making a draft
Recording away in a wise, old way.

A melancholic calm over the park, in which
He always writes, speaking as he goes, starting in a friendly tone
As if speaking to someone not there, which
Inevitably leads to a deflated sad monologue.

Recording the town and its people,
A paper, free for all, but not free of them.
Gossip and news, all important and trivial.
Hoped to be continued indefinitely.

Fearing the day, he will be forgotten,
For abandonment scars the heart,
The only words he never printed,
The last note from a spouse.

I had to do it for myself.

THESE BOOTS AREN'T MADE FOR RUNNING
BY AMIE LOCKWOOD

Sometimes when I'm hiking, I wonder why the fuck I'm hiking. Yet, when I reach the summit or end of the trail, I almost always wonder how I had the audacity to complain.

I can name at least six occasions where I threatened to pitch myself off the edge of a ridge because my thighs were burning.

I can picture tens of instances where I pictured giving up, heading back down the track, tossing my hiking boots into whatever beat-up car I was living in at the time, and never looking at a trail map again.

I can starkly recall screaming at the top of my lungs when my left calf muscle ripped while climbing an open cliff face on the Precipice Trail in Acadia National Park.

But, if we only remember the moments where we struggled and failed and worried and cried, we may never do anything at all.

When I was fourteen years old, I told my grandfather I was going to climb Everest one day. I had watched a documentary about three men achieving the incredible summit, and I wanted to do it too.

My grandfather died before he saw me reach the 8,849-metre summit, and I'll probably be dead before I see myself summit it too.

I am not made for mountains in the towering ranges of the Himalayas, but not in the same way I was never made for the small town where I grew up.

Which small town? no one may ask. Picture any small town in America where the high school sports team holds up the local community and more people believe in old legends than a woman's rights to her own body. Traditions die hard, and the locals die harder in the same bed where they've always slept surrounded by the same people they've always known.

No, I was never going to climb Everest, but I was never going to stay in Bumfuck Nowhere, USA, either.

When I turned eighteen, my momma took me aside in the kitchen of the small home that six of us shared and asked which college I'd be heading to in the fall.

Sometimes, when I think about the shock on her face when I said I wouldn't be going to college, I still feel sick. The way she opened her mouth and then closed it again, just managing to croak out the three syllables of my name before looking away — unfocused and gloomily across the dry plains and prairies of Bumfuck Nowhere.

That August, my twin brother headed to Northwestern, and I took Highway 20 and didn't look back. My parents had always preferred my brother anyway. He could hold up the weak foundations of our familial bonds from Evanston.

In not so many words, I ran away. In a few more words, I seized all of the doubt and uncertainty clawing at my brain, stuffed it into a duffel pack and a pair of hiking boots and headed for Appalachia.

The hiking boots were second-hand and peeling around the toes, but I felt strong when I pulled them on. Taller. Lighter. Ready to walk endlessly while trying to run away from the thoughts in my head.

But, it may come as no surprise that there's plenty of time to think while hiking. A poor Swedish man once found me braced against a tree on a trail in Mount Washington State Forest crying so hard that he'd asked if I'd been attacked. In the 'traditional' sense? No. Mentally? Yes. By fear of what lay ahead if I didn't find a more traditional path rather than the winding mountain trails? Definitely.

And sure, hiking boots are not made for running, but as I wore them in and made them my own, my concerns did seem to fall further behind. On the border of Virginia and North Carolina, I distinctly recall yelling at the Piedmont Mountains in the rear-view mirror that I would never settle for traditional. I would never let myself become stagnant. I would never settle for my perception of the mundane.

After my journey through Appalachia, I drove west. I sought out the Hoodoos in Bryce Canyon and sandstone cliffs in Zion then migrated south to Arizona for the winter. Days slipped by into weeks, and I continued to walk.

Some days I was exhausted before I'd even slipped out of my makeshift bed in the back of my van. Others, I was up before the sun with intent scorching in my veins. Regardless of how I felt when I woke up, I walked.

My body started to change. I shed weight from my stomach and thighs. The muscles in my calves became pronounced against my skin. The cheeks that my father had always pinched when I was younger thinned.

Beneath a sky full of stars in Joshua Tree, I took scissors to my dirty blonde hair and cut until I could feel the cool breeze on the back of my neck. The next afternoon, I met a young Austrian woman who was flying out of Los Angeles in three days. She sold me her almost new hiking boots for sixty dollars and a Chicago Blackhawks keyring.

At the summit of Ryan Mountain, overlooking the Pinto Basin and Lost Horse Valley, I took off my shabby hiking boots and set them carefully beside me. I brushed dust from the toe cap. For months, they had been my one constant. Letting go meant moving on from the shoes that had got me this far. At that moment, I felt as if I was saying goodbye to an old friend.

At that moment, I was also hit with a sinking loneliness. A loneliness that can't be filled by dark skies streaked with stars or the rich, fresh scent of Monterey Pine forests.

Looking out over the valleys below, I'd felt alone for the first time since leaving my childhood home. What had my mother been doing? Was my father still trying to finish his matchstick Chrysler Building? Had my brother finally found himself?

And that was how she found me, with a hand laid affectionately on my threadbare hiking boots and tears in my eyes, looking out over the California landscape.

By the time we reached the bottom of the winding trail, my new boots had given me a blister on each heel, but I hadn't stopped smiling. It wasn't until we reached the car park that she looked at me sheepishly, extended a chapped hand and told me her name.

Holly.

I told her mine and took her hand.

Without thinking, I followed her to her car.

Without thinking, I knew I'd follow her anywhere.

By fall, we'd covered hundreds of miles and got lost in the wilds of the Colorado Rockies. She was running from a failed marriage. I was slowing down to a jog from a life full of overbearing pressure and cookie-cutter expectations.

Together, we came to a steady jaunt along the banks of roaring rivers amongst soaring peaks and took seasonal jobs to tide us through until spring.

Sometimes, my mind would catch up to me, mostly in the moments when the world was quiet and when I could not see the never-ending wilderness that I was yet to explore.

On some days, it was darker than others. On the worst, it was as if I didn't know Holly at all.

But even on the darkest days, she'd stay.

She'd take my hands in hers, force my chin up to meet those kind brown eyes and whisper that the sun would rise again. It would rise again for us both.

Sometimes I still wonder if human beings are ever supposed to be alone. Solitude comes with a sense of liberation, but when we realise the extent of our isolation, its depth is frightening.

For the first time, as spring came to the Rocky Mountains, I craved the path that would lead me home. I wouldn't run back, but I would make it a destination. A new summit to reach that stretched out before us with uncomfortable uncertainty.

I remember the concern on her face when I told her. She was unusually quiet for a long while. I fell for her all over again as I watched the morning light flit across her eyes.

"Where you go," She'd said after a long while, chewing on her thumbnail. "I go."

Without Holly, I never would have made the journey home. The sleepless nights in Nebraska. The argument in Missouri that was resolved with a can of root beer. The sickening but desperate desire to perform a U-turn on Highway 20 and not pass into the town limits of Bumfuck Nowhere.

It surprised me most of all how willingly I crossed the threshold of my childhood home and tumbled into my momma's arms.

It did not surprise me that my parents took to Holly as easily as I had.

When we departed two weeks later, I promised my momma we'd be back as soon as we could.

And as Holly had promised, the sun rose again that day and the days that followed. We fell into a routine, working for a few months and then travelling for a few more. We visited my parents when we could, and we bought a bigger van. We headed to Europe and walked the Rota Vicentina Fisherman's Trail in Portugal then the Rätikon Alps High Trail through Austria and Switzerland.

On the third day of our agonising route through the Zillertal Alps, I starkly recall looking over at Holly's expression of determination and gritted teeth as we climbed. I knew by then that escaping to the mountains no longer felt like running. It was still arduous and difficult, but the sense that I was heading simply toward a goal rather than away from a frightening apprehension made me feel lighter.

In late fall that year, we headed to Canada and spent our hours in front of a log fire when we weren't hiking or working.

On New Year's Day, as we emerged spluttering and laughing from a freezing and very brief swim in Horseshoe Lake, I'd looked at Holly with determination in my eyes.

I'd almost bottled it and blamed it on my chattering teeth before hardening my resolve and whispering, "Please marry me".

Somehow not to my surprise, she said yes.

We married in the summer surrounded by our few friends and fewer family members. My brother, a recent graduate from Northwestern, walked Holly up the aisle. The sky became a spectacular orange and rouge as the sun sank lower. The whole night, I watched Holly shine. A lantern in the darkest cave. The most spectacular dawn after a night ravaged by storm.

We honeymooned in Badlands National Park and spoke of everything we knew about ourselves and one another. Solitude may come with a sense of liberation, but being with Holly filled me with a strong feeling of freedom.

With Holly, it felt like I could stop running at last.

For months, life had a quality about it that I'd never experienced before. The edges of every memory seemed to sparkle. Each moment was vivid and vibrant.

Although there is more to life than love, I've always felt that it is our ability to love so passionately or viciously that defines us. Whether we experience or incite heartbreak or inspire adoration, the people we love somehow underpin everything we do.

At that time, every decision I made seemed fuelled by thoughts of my wife and family. I had a life of my own to shape and a path of my own to take. A path I could experience at my own pace with my love at my side.

And then, it felt like I could not move at all.

Almost three years after we married, Holly suffered a severe brain haemorrhage and passed away in hospital. I was by her side as she passed, her chapped fingers laced through my own.

It felt then, and still feels now, like I lost a huge part of myself that day.

But, somehow, the sun still rises — just as she promised it would.

And she would never have wanted me to forget that when the world was darkest.

So sometimes when I'm hiking, I wonder why the fuck I still hike.

I can name at least seven occasions where I threatened to chuck myself into a crevice because my legs ached, and Holly told me I was being ridiculous.

I can picture tens of instances where I wanted to give up, head back down the track and toss my hiking boots away for good, but Holly would always remind me how worth it the whole thing would be once we got to the top of the slope.

I can starkly recall crying for hours when I thought I'd never heal from the pressures I'd faced and the worry I'd felt.

Somewhere along the trail, with Holly's deep eyes full of sunshine and her smile full of joy, that all slipped away.

The Snake
by Martin Ansell

She lies on a lie and dreams of the truth
But forgets it whenever she wakes,
She rests in a nest of forgotten hope
And is slowly consumed by the snake.

His wishes are hisses whispered in ear
And she fights to block out his charms,
But they penetrate deep beyond her defence
We can tell by the cuts on her arms.

She sings in her sleep a song of despair
He coils tightly denying her voice,
A ballard of tears rain down her sweet face
But he bites and poisons her choice.

This time a change - resistance is clear
Now immune to his poisonous dose,
She pulls the snake near, and whispers in ear
"My love, why don't you come close."

She wakes with a start, his spell fades away
The snake slithers back to his side,
She reaches and grabs the steel by her bed
And makes herself shoes from his hide.

DEATH

decease | murder | finality

death (noun)

1. *the fact of someone dying or being killed*

2. *the end of life; the state of being dead*

THE ENGLISH COLLECTIVE

A Pandemic Funeral
by Billie-Martha Newland

Darkness descends, not of night but of a forever sleep.
Spirits fill the room before descending to the afterlife.
I think about when you told me the story of Little Bo Peep.
Five people sit on benches six feet apart, accompanied by bibles and masks.

Ironic, isn't it? Six feet apart before burying you six feet under.
In the new world, only five are allowed to go to funerals.
My sister video calls me, blurred as the signal comes and goes.
I look at the maroon coffin on the podium with a crimson curtain surrounding it as I pick at my cuticles.

"We'll meet again, don't know where, don't know when"
Vera Lynn reassures me that this is not the end.
The time has come to say our final goodbyes.
Slowly, the veil to the other side starts to close and the priest says his final words.

My family are ushered out ready for the next unfortunate family to say their goodbyes to their loved one.
And just like that, a 20-year memory. Gone

Deep Rooted
by Carlie Wells

Thick sludge covered uneven ground as harsh winds battered the lone tree. Once part of a great forest, now reduced to the singular oak, its branches bare and bending beneath the elements, the bark was torn, and the roots exposed. A once thriving nest, now tethered within the branches, void of all life, there would be no chicks this year and perhaps none the year after. Despite all this Charlie loved the tree. In some perhaps silly kind of way, it gave him hope. Despite barely being a shell of itself it still stood strong. He liked to think that if he got home, he too could stand strong. And if he couldn't get home, he'd like to lay under it as he died. A morbid thought perhaps, but it could very well be his reality after all it was Ben's. Ben whose hand he had cradled as his blood gushed into the ground just this morning. Ben who had a smile that could make a man laugh on even the bleakest of days. Ben who had now gone, leaving behind a girl at home who had been awaiting his return.

The sun glared harshly through the splattering of the clouds, but it gave no relief from the cold embrace of winter. Its rays glinted harshly off from the bronze buttons despite most of them being covered in a thick layer of grime... Well that was nothing new, everything was covered in some kind of muck that Charlie really did not want to think about. And that was the key to surviving, not thinking about it. Just do. Just do. And if he ignored the way his hands shook as he took a smoke, then that was his problem.

He turned and began his way back to the valley forge, his boots squelching in the thick mud that consumed everything, although nature was trying to prevail. It was seen in the sprouts of grass that shot up only to be trampled back down to earth. Ironically, he wondered if blood was a good fertiliser, it would certainly seem so. He was greeted by Tucker as he ducked into his tent. Tucker was a lean boy, and Charlie called him a boy because he simply was one, eighteen and straight from the farm he called home. His ginger hair and green uniform caused a striking contrast, and his constant chatter caused him many an earache, but it served as a distraction, at least that's what he told himself as his eyes continued to stray to the unmade bunk that was… used to be Ben's. It would be filled soon, a fresh recruit with an ill-fitting uniform and a yearning to be part of the action. He used to be that way, he was proud to wear his uniform and eager to show the enemy that they would not be taken. But seeing his brothers die one by one hadn't left much of that eager green boy left. Instead, he counted the days as good and bad days. Today had not been a good day.

"Did ya see the new red cross girls?" grinned Tucker as he used a match to light up a smoke before passing another one to him. He ran a hand through his thick brown hair as he grinned back. "And you think, they will want a squirt like you?" Tucker elbowed him, as they shared a laugh together.

After a few games of Blackjack which Tucker lost consistently, he quit, but not before losing two packs of smokes. Those were like finding gold, a man's currency out here. Although, he mused as he placed his pack behind his head, he did know guys who dug for gold, after all a golden tooth from a German was still worth its weight in pounds.

Charlie closed his eyes, as the wind battered the tent. It was not comfortable by any means but compared to the frozen ground outside it was a luxury, one not often given. With the howling of the wind, Charlie could almost picture home. The smell of whiskey, the roaring of an open hearth and freshly-baked bread which Mr Applebee sold in the shop a few doors down. Charlie was dirt poor and he knew it. He'd worked in the factories from a young age and often ran around shoeless once he'd worn down his old ones but he was street smart and he made enough money to support his parents and sister who were still across the vast ocean and although he had never been further from home right now, as he drifted into sleep, he had never felt closer.

Charlie couldn't say what woke him, it could have been the tent canopy that caved in on top of him, or it could have been the screams of the dead. More likely, it was the motors exploding all around him. An explosion threw him off of his feet and his back crashed into the side of a tent pole causing pain to radiate throughout. His vision swam as he scrambled back to his feet as he gripped his rifle, a hand latched into his arm as he was pulled upright by an ash covered Tucker. He had a cut running down the side of his face and his lips set in a grim line.

"You alright?" Tucker asked.

Charlie nodded, "Let's go."

They ventured out from the broken tent and walked into a battlefield. The glow of the full moon had nothing on the roaring flames that licked dangerously into the night. Men were rolling on the ground in a desperate attempt to put out flames that wanted to devour them. The shrieking of shells cut through the smoke as more smoke and flames grew. They ran towards the command tents, trying to find an officer. They had no idea where the Germans would be advancing from. Tucker tripped beside him and fell to the ground landing in a muddy puddle.

"Come on," urged Charlie as he tried to pull Tucker up. He didn't move. "Tucker." Desperation and pleading fell from his tongue as he crouched down and saw the neat bullet hole decorating the back of his chest.

With shaking hands, he turned him over and saw the glazed look that covered his unseeing eyes as red bloomed from his chest. Charlie's chest constricted as tears threatened to fall. Not another, he had lost too many friends and yet, as his hands slid in the blood that leaked into the puddle below, he found he could do nothing. He should move, he hadn't seen where the bullet had come from, and yet he couldn't. A shell landed near, and the blast threw him away from Tucker. And this time the blood was coming from him. The pain was blinding at first but as Charlie tried to move, it turned almost warm. Red. Red was everywhere. The sky was cast in the shadows of the flames. The ground was red with his own blood this time and his uniform was saturated in it. His hands grasped at something, at anything and yet all they found was more red. Charlie turned his head and, in the distance, he could see the tree.

The tree still stood, smoke obstructed his view, but it was all he could see. The branches bounced in the blast as the ground shook and trembled around him, a branch snapped and he swore he could hear the creak it gave before falling. His vision began to darken as the shells began to stop but the tree was still there. The branch still falling,
falling,
falling,
falling,
and landing, with a soft thud.

Deforestation Exploitation
by Shannon Oliver

Where do you go,
Once you have been destroyed?
Where do you go,
Once only your end remains?

All you have to offer,
Taken for another's gain.
Left a lightweight shell
No use as you are.

You could be sent back to your beginning,
To grow and be removed again.
Or you could be transformed into glamour
Exploited for unnecessary luxury.

The branches you carried so tenderly,
Snapped and taken from you.
Leaves of vibrant colours and unique shapes
Gone within an instant.

And as I hold your broken body close,
I wonder where you'll go.
What will happen to the memories we made,
And will you ever come back home?

Elizabeth's Lover
by Emily Nunan

The wind whipped Elizabeth's hair wildly around her face, the air smelled of salt. The sea pushed against the ship causing friction between the sides of the vessel and the ongoing storm. A thousand barnacles stuck to the ship, sucking on to the wood for dear life.

The men and children ran around the deck grabbing and pulling at the ropes to keep the sails in sync with the roaring wind. The captain called for all the men to heave and pull harder, the boat rocked to one side, slightly tipping into the next wave. Elizabeth rushed for her lover: Caspian, calling him to hold her one last time before they both sank to their deaths. He refused her, claiming his duty lay with his ship and crewmen and turned her away. Her heart plummeted into her stomach, her insides turning.

Elizabeth sucked in a deep breath holding on to her tears, she knew this day would come, she saw it in her dreams. She didn't think it would come true. She knew what she had to do.

She effortlessly stepped out of her heels, she pulled at her dress trying to make it less tight. The cream corset pushed into her ribs, restricting her breathing. Elizabeth looked at the horizon, the one she had stared at for the past year. The sun started to break away from where the sea met the ocean, the orange and reds dancing in both sky and sea making the whole world twirl in a volcanic rush.

Elizabeth had faith in her dreams, that she would be rescued by an unstoppable force. A force that held her in its arms when she descended into the afterlife. She saw something circling the ship. A large dark shadow. She knew she had angered the gods for being with Caspian in this life. Her father had forbidden it but she never listened, she followed her heart and now it was snapped in two.

Caspian was a God: a creature of the night. He needed the life of an innocent soul. He knew Elizabeth was destined for greater things, she was special.

Elizabeth looked toward her captain, her lover one last time before her eyes fell shut and the wind carried her off the ship. She plunged deep down into the darkness. The icy water gilded around her body and pulled her further into the world of the unknown.

The black shadow vanished from the ocean, nowhere in sight. Something grabbed hold of Elizabeth's feet, she started to panic, she thrashed around to get to the surface but something kept pulling her down. Little ripples of light twirled around her, she reached out to touch them. She felt nothing in return. The water forced its way into her system, taking control, breaking her down bit by bit.

Elizabeth knew her time was coming to an end. She glanced at the surface. The ship sailed away without her. The thought of death didn't scare her, just the thought of not one person remembering her. Her family that she left behind, the friends she ignored and her lover that froze her still beating heart.

Elizabeth would die in the arms of her provider, surrounded by darkness that her lover created. Caspian the creation of darkness.

Execution
by Billie-Martha Newland

I saw the tragic departure of my generation destroyed,
How I mourned the disappearance.
Are you upset about how tragical it is?
Does it tear you apart to see the disappearance so sad?
Never forget the tragic disappearance of our old world.
Pay attention to the execution,
The execution is the cruellest process of all
Does the execution make you shiver? Does it?
In the distance, my family stand facing the audience of soldiers,
side by side.
Holding hands, tears fall from their bloodshot, black, sunken
eyes.
Screeching missiles fall miles behind them,
The smoke fills the air, I am blinded.
"ready, aim, fire".
My family are dead.
A war for nothing.

FORESTS
BY ERICA FOSTER

The world will know the peace that is given by the forest: a
deafening and needing silence.
the birds, the woods, the walks.
Away from the noise and stress of lives.
We have taken. held. Formed.
There should be a day that we love the forest.
That day should turn into a week, into a month, into a year, then
two and then realise that the forest is a part of humanity.
The trees have faces. names, thoughts and feelings
they taste the ash on their tongues. Feel it in their eyes,
they see the destruction;
Humans murdering their brothers and sisters, siblings; mothers
and fathers.
their shields made of bark won't protect their hearts; it won't stop
the carvings of their names;
as the life is taken from their eyes.
As the armies fall.
One by one.

Lamb
by Amy Butler

Lights splashed in the street where Martha stood. Laughter and music fought their way through the door of the club. The doors crashed open, and two men pushed past her. She stared dumbly and apologised under her breath. Then looked back up at the flashing sign which marked the building as the sort of establishment her mother would disapprove of.

Carmen was waiting inside, waiting for her. But Martha hesitated, frozen. She couldn't bring herself to go inside, but she couldn't go home either.

There was a dead man on her couch.

Carmen kept her eye on the entrance, twirling a cherry in the cocktail she wasn't planning on drinking. The waitress, Audrey, leant over the bar towards her.

"You been here a while. You waiting for someone?" she asked.

Carmen smirked.

"Just a little friend," she replied.

Audrey's smile darkened, but her eyes lit up.

"That so? Something the rest of us might want in on?"

She spotted her tiptoeing girl through the crowd. Could smell her stale, flowery perfume.

"Audrey, hon, I think the boys in the kitchen needed you. Why don't you go check that," she said without taking her eyes off Martha.

Huffing, she did as she was told. Rising from her chair, she sauntered through the crowd to meet her.

"Hey, honey, I almost figured you weren't gonna come," she crooned.

Martha caught her eyes and beamed up at her, overwhelmed by the relief of a familiar
Face.

"Of course, I was gonna," she mumbled. "Can you help me, Carmen? I mean will you really..."

Tucking a stray hair behind her ear, Carmen leaned in close. Her face was so warm against her icy hand. Martha went silent.

"Of course, you poor thing. Now let's sort this whole mess out..."

PROTEST POEM
BY HOLLY-MAY BROADLEY-DARBY

The earth was once growing strong and tall,
waking up when the birds sang their call.
Nature was the sound that woke the earth,
as it heard their cry before their birth.

As nature's newborn begins to crawl,
weeping tears of sorrow as they fall.
With raging fires burning through the lands,
is this what the human race had planned?

Around the last tree, they form a bond,
joining as one but do we respond?
We just stand by and watch as they die.
They'll be gone in a blink of an eye!

Replaced
by Megan Goff

He says he's sorry about five times a month, but he never changes. Always sorry for the same reasons but makes no move to fix it. He makes a court-ordered effort about once a month to actually see me, in hopes I'd have changed, that I'd be less mouthy this time around. It's a vicious cycle. I will never fit into his vision of a perfect daughter, and I will make no move to fix this. Why should I have to change if he doesn't? I used to want nothing more than for him to like me, I used to fantasise about him coming running back to me apologising profusely for every mean thing he'd ever said to me, that he'd be a stable and reassuring presence in my life for once. We'd go on holidays, and picnics. I'd have my own room at his place, and he would decorate it just how I'd like it and he'd do this all because he loved me.

Now, I only fantasise about hurting him back, about drawing the apology from him in new and exciting ways each time. I will never be the sweet, innocent little girl he wanted me to be and there was no one to blame for that but him. He made me angry. He made me who I am.

Today was one of his court-ordered visits, he was coming to my mother's house again and we'd sit in the garden in awkward silence for about an hour and he'd leave again. It was the same every month. Soon enough I'd be eighteen and able to make the decision for myself to permanently cut him out but in the meantime, I had to appease my mother's desire for me to try and form a bond. She is worried my lack of a father figure would mess up my head permanently, she worries a lot.

I fussed about pretending to be using the bathroom when he arrived, the more time I spent in here the less I had to spend out there, with him. I took as long as humanly possible to tie up my boots before heading outside where I could see the back of his balding head from where he sat, slouched, at the patio table. Mum hovered in the kitchen whispering encouragements to me before hurrying away to her bedroom. She kept an eye through her window that looked out upon the garden, sneaking glances every ten minutes in hopes she'd find us bonding, talking, anything but staring blankly at each other as I shot down any attempt at any conversation he started. That's just how it always went?

His expression turned nervous as he saw me approaching, which was not a good sign. The only other time I'd seen him so apprehensive was when he first told me about Malory. Malory was his new girlfriend; one I was sure to like much more than the last whore. Dad made a lot of assumptions about my reaction; he made a lot of assumptions about me. He didn't know me at all.

"Good morning, Charlotte. How are you?"

He waited for an answer that never came. The atmosphere tilted, uneasy from the second I walked out. Nothing new.

Sometimes I wonder if I'm doing too much. I think about Mum and her sad face when we finish yet another unproductive visit. Sometimes I wonder how she can bear to have him in her house, in her garden, talking to her daughter after everything he did to her. I look at him with his fancy suit and carefully styled hair, I smell the cigarette smoke that wafts from him with every turn of the wind. He once told me I was the reason he smoked, that I was so difficult to love that it turned him to an old addiction. I think he just likes to blame me for everything that's wrong with his life. Better to have a difficult daughter than to be a shit dad.

"Okay, I'll get straight to it. I have some news."

He paused, leaving gaps he knew I would never fill.

"Me and Malory are having a baby. And I've asked her to marry me."

For once I'm compelled to actually answer him, except I can't form a proper sentence. Thoughts flying through my head so fast it just sounds like buzzing, the only clear words I can form are:

"What the fuck!" It comes out as a shout.

Dad looks taken aback, physically recoiling from me as if I had spat at him. The thought was tempting.

"I know it may come as a surprise; we don't talk about Malory much but-"

"We barely talk at all."

"I have a lot of regrets with how I handled our relationship after I ended things with your mother. But I want that to change, Malory would really like to get to know you, and for you to get to know the new baby."

"Oh, so that's what this is about! This isn't you trying to fix things, you're being forced into it!"

"That's not fair, Charlotte."

"How isn't it fair? It's the truth, no?"

The whirlwind in my head just keeps getting faster, harsher, building up to a hurricane. It's torpedoed everything else; I can think of nothing except how angry I am, and how much I want him to hurt the way he keeps hurting me.

Dad was still blabbering on, but I wasn't listening. My mind raced too fast, I couldn't process anything he was doing or saying. The thought of him having another child. The thought of him treating that child the way he treats me. It made me livid. Worse, the thought of him treating that child better, that I was just a mistake to be learned from. His trial run at being a father before he committed properly to his new child, and to Malory. The fantasies about holidays, picnics, the lovingly decorated bedroom in his house, the father that would give me the world no questions asked, robbed from me, and bestowed upon this new child. It didn't deserve it. I deserved it.

I never understood what I did to make him hate us so much, when talking to me became such a chore for him, such a burden. There are so many pictures of the two of us from when I was a baby and a toddler. He used to look at me so lovingly, a stark contrast to the guilt-ridden look of disdain of the present.

The fantasies of hurting him play in my mind, fantasies of making him scream in pain. And I'm moving before I even register where I'm going. He's still talking, calling after me in an attempt to talk it out. He doesn't love me, and he never will. He wants to make me watch as he gives this child everything he denied me, as he treats Malory with all the love and respect he denied my mother.

I'm in the kitchen. He's not far behind me following me inside. Blood is rushing in my ears so loud, and my heart is beating so aggressively. I still can't hear a word he's saying. I look down and there's a knife in my hand. He's yelling now, I can hear my mother's footsteps banging down the stairs. There's blood on his shirt. There's blood everywhere. Blood on his fancy suit, in his carefully styled hair. He's on the floor now, my mother is here. She's screaming, sobbing. Why she would cry over this man is beyond me. He was replacing us; he was never going to treat us with respect. Why should I treat him with any? I see it now, so clearly, this was the only way this was ever going to end. The vicious cycle of empty apologies and broken promises, I had to be the one to break it.

Mum's left the kitchen. I think she's on the phone. The blood rushing through my head has started to subside now as I regain full consciousness of my surroundings. I hear my mother mention the word police, I can hear her sobs. Blood pools around my feet. Oh, God. I didn't notice the way his chest was heaving until it stopped, the way he was panting and screaming until he was silent. I find I miss the noise; it was distracting. Now it's quiet and everything's real. I've killed my dad.

I think about running but a sudden wave of exhaustion takes over and I fall to my knees. My face feels wet but I'm unsure as to whether it's tears or my father's blood. What have I done? I've ruined my mother's life. She'll be all alone after they take me away, I wonder how often they'll let her visit me. The thought of her alone worries me, but the thought of me in prison terrifies me. I wonder if she'll move on. If she too will start a new family without me. I think I might be the problem?

The Bread One
by Emily Nunan

Flying over the station and my mind instantly goes back to that night. The night I killed my friend: Meg.

She was in the biggest state I had ever witnessed from her. Crying and screaming at me for buying brown bread instead of white. I'm sorry for what I did but she got what was coming to her. Let's be real, brown bread is much healthier. You know what I say, 'white makes you wanna fight', and that's what she did. She fought for hours, until I stuffed her with her stupid white bread.

You better enjoy your bread, Meg.

THE BREAD ONE INSPIRED
ASSAULT WITH A BREADLY WEAPON
BY MARTIN ANSELL

Claire smiled as she watched the birds feed. It made her happy to watch the sparrows flit between the feeders and scraps she had put out on the lush green lawn. Four of the feathered friends were chirruping as they fed on something she had put out after the police had left.

They'd found her room-mate's body. Her head had been caved in with what they suspected to be an iron bar. They had no suspects.

She wondered how long the sparrows would take to eat the baguette she had left out.

And whether it would thaw before they finished.

THE BREAD ONE INSPIRED
BREAD & BREAKFAST
BY NICK GEORGE

Owning the farmhouse on Gold Hill was a dream come true. I'd needed this; it was more than just a home. 'Pumpernickel' was perfect, although refurbishing the crusty old cottage to create the B&B had taken all my dough.

With everything to prove and hungry for success, I didn't loaf about. Despite my great taste and appetite for DIY, it took a gruelling twelve (or thirteen?) months. Like artisan bakers handcrafting focaccia, I took pride in my work, something I'd inherited from my mother.

With a wry smile I welcomed my first guests, raising the bread knife behind them.

The End of a Friend
by Billie-Martha Newland

They say, all good things must end,
I think about you every night.
A dream washed away by time, "Don't mourn for me" you say.
I shed a tear on the darkness, your voice torments my mind, but to what end?

They say, all good things must end,
I am but a flower, wilted and dead.
I'll hold your hand forever you said,
You slip away, lying in your eternal bed.

I pray every night as hopelessness eats me,
The anguish within my soul torments.
"Why did you have to leave?" I say lying next to your tree.
The shadows are my only companion, for darkness is my only friend.

They say, all good things must end,
We are just flowers, wilted and dead.

THE ENGLISH COLLECTIVE

THE WINDOWS TO THE SOUL
BY CARLIE WELLS

They say that the eyes are the gateway into a person's soul and that you can tell what kind of individual they are just by looking into their eyes.

Amy's eyes had been clear blue. They had shone in the light and were bright and happy.

Well, that was until they had been plucked from their sockets like one would pluck a fresh grape. Her eyes were laid about a foot from her body, perfectly round and undamaged. If one was to look close enough at the now murky pupils, you could almost see the terror they must have held, the horrors they must have seen. Perhaps it was a mercy they had been the first to be mutilated. At least Amy didn't have to see what was coming next, even if she would surely have felt it.

Beth's eyes had almost been identical to the damp moss that they had been delicately placed on, much like a tiny nest holding two valuable little eggs. Unlike Amy, the eyes hadn't been the first to be mutilated. That honour had gone to her fingers, which had been chopped at the knuckle and piled meticulously on top of one another, a perverted Jenga.

But these eyes, the ones Philip was staring into, were so much worse. Dark, endless tunnels with no end and no beginning.

There was no warmth here, and he doubted there ever would be. These were the eyes of a sadistic killer, who got off on mutilating young women. He had a preference for blondes; he'd leave their hair splayed out, a mockery of a halo, and the only part left untouched.

That didn't mean that he hadn't gone for brunettes or redheads. Megan had been a redhead, and they had found her right foot a few metres from her body. The coroner's report and forensics discovered that she had been made to drag herself along the forest floor after it had been hacked off.

The scene played over and over in Philip's head. He could almost imagine how terrified Megan would have been, how she would have known she didn't have long left. She had been left to bleed out, and the ground was saturated in her blood, the grass stained a vibrant red.

He'd been the first on the scene, driving back from Cassie's school where he'd given a speech about working in the force, accompanied by the usual safety talks. He visited Oak Moor Academy a lot, as he always did the school run unless he was called away on a case. The idea of Cassie walking alone, especially in the December evenings when it would be dark before she made it home, didn't sit right with him. So, he made the effort to run her backwards and forwards.

Philip also helped with the junior football team. He'd played as a teen and closely followed the sport, so it wasn't a bother to help out, especially since Adam, the coach, had sprained his ankle while putting the Christmas tree up. How Adam had managed that, Philip didn't know, but he didn't want the team to miss out on valuable practice before matches.

Abby, Adams's daughter also helped, as she was on her university summer break and had played football through her society. Being within the killer's age range and a natural blonde, she'd been especially rattled by all the killings which had been shaking the city to its core. She never went anywhere alone, which is why Philip often drove her home after practice was finished. He'd stop by and have a quick cup of tea with Adam afterwards, and then head on home in time for dinner.

Phillip loved Cassie, he really did. He was at every ballet show, paid for her horse riding lessons, and even knew all the words to The Lion King, which had been watched non-stop over the last few months. But Philip would have loved to have a son, too. A son to follow in his footsteps, who would want to play sports, and who Philip could teach to shave and buy his first beer on his eighteenth.

It wasn't to be. Laura, his wife of ten years, had suffered complications bringing Cassie into the world and he had almost lost them both. Philip had spent weeks between the NICU and intensive care, scared out of his mind. It had been a miracle that they had both pulled through, but there would be no more red-faced newborns in the Maxwell household. Cassie was to be their only child. Laura had cried once the reality set in, blaming herself for not taking it easy, for insisting she hadn't needed bed rest and continuing to go about as normal, despite the doctors advising not to. For a short while, Philip had blamed her a little too, but every time her hazel eyes would fill with unfallen tears, and she would grip him just that little bit tighter, he found he couldn't truly blame her for it. It wasn't her fault, not really.

Behind the glass, the monster smirked at him, as if he could read Philip's thoughts.

'Monster' summed this being up, for sure, he could not truly be a man or even human after the acts he had committed. Maddie wasn't supposed to be a perverted gallery piece that only the twisted could understand, she was supposed to be starting her dream job as a vet. Her parents had gone into detail about her love of animals, and how she was a gentle soul who was loved by everyone. Instead, she had been victim number four and had to be identified through her fingerprints. There hadn't been much left of her face after it had been carefully peeled from her skull.

Mark was still staring back through the glass.

Philip didn't like to use the monster's name. In fact, he actively tried not to. It seemed too human, something this thing was not. Each woman had been horrifically tortured, each mutilated in ways completely different, completely unique. It was almost like he had been experimenting, trying to find what worked for him, and there hadn't been a stone that Mark had not turned over. Mark would never leave any DNA at the scene, and everything had been sterilised in a cheap household bleach that could be found in most stores.

The one constant was the eyes. They had always been gently eased from their sockets and placed delicately away from the body, almost as if Mark was trying to protect them, that he didn't want to look into them as he committed his sick acts. To the rational mind, the sane mind, this made no sense, but Philip was certain that in Mark's it was perfectly logical.

Philip, as much as he tried to deny it, had become obsessed with the case. His team had been put in charge, but even as more bodies turned up, there still hadn't been many leads, so he would always be found in front of the board that displayed what little they did have. He interviewed every suspect, every witness. Mark had been a ghost for a long time, and although they only had four official victims, Philip just knew that there would be many more. Serial killers didn't just start with this level of mutilation, it was built up over time. Had Mark just grown lazy with disposing of the bodies, or was he toying with the police, playing his own cat and mouse game?

"Dad? Dinner's ready."

Cassie's voice shook Philip from his thoughts. He sighed as he splashed his face with water and gazed back up at the mirror.

Mark was smiling now, all teeth. A vicious kind of thing.

To Leave the Pages
by Carlie Wells

To see oneself displayed in a novel is fascinating, reading thoughts and expressions which have been placed upon paper. Your very being concluded to a few sentences. For my heartbreak to be displayed both so wonderfully and cruelly. My love with Henry was filled with torment and joy. An everlasting contradiction. For us, love took not one form but two.

For love is a shapeshifter, never appearing in the same form twice. Sometimes it starts as a small shoot in the ground, slowly growing beneath the warm rays of the sun before blooming into a ruby rose with silken petals. Magnificently, it stands, the jewel of any garden. A marvel to gaze upon and tantalising sweet to your senses. This love is gentle, whispered promises of forever and stolen kisses in the twilight. The kiss on the back of a lady's hand, a handpicked daisy in bloom. It's a love that slowly consumes your heart. The fresh summer's day, the glow of the candlelight, the rose blush that dusts your cheek as a dimpled smile is flashed cheekily. Youthful and filled with longing. Feeling as though you're a princess in a castle with a charming prince coming with a declaration that he will love you forever. Oh, how I longed for this love, to dally in the throes of this succulent passion. Content till the end of my days, how could I need anything else when my prince charming invaded my senses? Dreary grey, replaced with dazzling colour.

But the reality, oh the reality. Was not what I so wished for but rather became my worst nightmare.

For within his grasp was a beating heart. My beating heart, which I had given him freely. To cherish, to treasure, to love. Alas, gone were his lingering caresses or soothing touches. Now, all that clung to him was the unfathomable truth. A truth which wretched at my very soul. I was nothing. A passing fancy I may have been but never his princess. There was no blazing stallion coming, just broken dreams. His once honey-laced words now dripped with poison on newly sharpened teeth. Cheeky smiles replaced mockingly with a vicious snarl. A blackness had settled over his once warm hazel eyes filled with nothing but deep hatred. Cold hands wretched at my heart until it shattered into a million pieces and fell at his feet. Spitting and snarling he tore into my soul, a once blooming rose wilting into ash with blood dripping from newly sharpened thrones. For life, as much as we deny it is the most beautiful lie, while death is the most devastating truth. For how could I go back to a life in the dark? A life without him was nothing. I was nothing. Just a foolish girl clinging to an unthinkable dream, a dream which would never bear the succulent fruit I so very wished for.

For upon my lap, was this very story. The story of the heart of Samantha Lee. The story of how I died.

WITCH IN THE WOOD
BY MEGAN GOFF

We had set out roughly two hours ago, wandering the quiet roads of the Cotswolds with Nadia keeping a firm grasp on the map and compass before deciding to take a shortcut through a small forest. The path inside was winding and the bushes on either side were thick and stuffed full of stinging nettles and blackberries. The trees got thicker as we walked further in, to the point where we could no longer see the sky, just a few rays of sunshine peeking through the gaps in the leaves. The shade was a welcome reprieve from the open fields where the sun beat down on us mercilessly.

We decided to take our lunch break in one of the clearings that seemed to be dotted along the path in a regular pattern, most likely cleared by the council to accommodate hikers and cyclists. It was a circular patch of grass with a small pond situated at the very back, almost hidden in the tall wall of grass that grew around the entire area like some sort of natural fence.

"This place is, like, magical." Olivia gushed, throwing herself and her backpack down on the soft bed of clovers.

We sat in a vague attempt at a circle and ate our packed lunches in a joyful quiet until we heard someone approaching.

Curious we all paused our eating, waiting for whoever was approaching to come close enough.

"Hey, isn't that Lilly? Where's her group?"

She hadn't noticed us yet, still a ways down the cycle path, tears streaming down her face, loose strands of bright ginger hair sticking to her sweaty forehead and cheekbones. Nadia called out to her. She startled, recognition washed over her face, smoothing out her furrowed brows and pursed lips, her entire body sagged with obvious relief at finding us. She began to sprint, arriving before us in a matter of seconds. I had no idea anyone could run that fast. She collapsed onto her knees on the foliage in front of our group, her sobbing intensified and she started rambling.

"I just stopped to drink some water, I don't know how they walked away that quickly, I looked back up and they were just gone."

"Your group? They're gone?"

"I don't know!" Lilly kept wailing, the sound seemed almost inhuman.

Esther rubbed reassuring circles on her back. "We'll keep an eye out for them as we walk but they've probably walked onto the next checkpoint to find a teacher when they couldn't find you," she said trying to come up with an explanation.

Lilly seemed to have calmed down a little now she knew she wasn't alone.

We walked on, and Lilly's sniffling quietened down to nothing. Time seemed to drag as we kept on for what felt like an eternity. There was a large bird's nest tucked into the branches of one particularly large tree, the small chirps of birds sounded out from within it.

"Are we sure it should be taking this long?" Jamie was peering over Nadia's shoulder at the map.

"It's not been that long, don't be dramatic." Nadia snapped.

"Did anyone check the time as we came in?" I piped in.

"I- can't remember," Nadia stopped abruptly, the rest of us tripped over ourselves to not crash into her. "I swear I checked the time."

"These things happen, Nadia," Esther comforted as she huddled around the map.

Ahead of us, there was another clearing identical to the others that lined the cycle path. Pointing towards it I suggested, "Let's stop there. Regain our bearing and write down the time on the corner of the map so we can keep track."

The clearing was the same shape and size as the one we had stopped in for lunch. To avoid the tense feeling amongst the rest of the group I walked around the perimeter examining the different leaves and flowers dotting the large bush of plants. At the very back of the clearing I noticed the foliage thinned enough you could walk through it, on the other side sat a small circular pond around a metre wide with small clumps of plants littering the surface. I took a moment of peace, peering into the water as I saw small fish swimming under the surface.

As I reached down to run my fingertips across the surface I noticed the reflection was unnaturally clear. Looking closer I realised the skin of the hand in the reflection was wrinkled and baggy, covered in warts and calluses. The sounds of the forest fell away as I leaned down to examine it, the birds and the wind both eerily silent. A haggard face jumped at me, trapped within the water, silently screaming as it pounded its hand reaching out of the water.

I screamed as I scrambled back, away from the pond. The sounds of the birds and the wind and the voices of the other girls returned all at once, only rivalled by the noise of my heart beating in my ears. Adrenaline pushed me through the grass boundary surrounding the clearing and straight into Esther, knocking us both over.

"Jesus, Cassie! What's wrong with you?" Nadia yelled.

"The - the pond. And there was a hand and an old lady." I screamed tugging on Esther's arm in an attempt to get them all moving. They all just sat staring at me. "COME ON!"

"Cassie, what the fuck are you talking about?" Esther looked at me like I was crazy, eyebrow furrowed and lips pursed.

Nadia stood from where she had been resting and marched over to the pond.

"NO! Nadia don't go near it, there's a face in the pond!"

"You're acting nuts, Cassie, get a grip." She batted the tall plants away to reveal the pond. But no hand reaching out from the depths. Nadia walked closer and looked down at the surface.

"I don't see a hand. Are you sure it wasn't just your reflection?" She asked in a patronising tone.

"I am sure! It was old and wrinkly. Like an old lady."

"Sure there was, we're not gonna fall for this prank, Cassie." Jamie laughed.

"I don't know guys. These woods are seriously creepy." Olivia's voice sounded shaky, and she started edging away from the back of the clearing onto the path, not taking her eyes off the pond.

"Oh, don't be stupid Olivia. There was not an old lady in the pond." Nadia spun around to glare at Olivia.

"Let's just keep walking." Lilly seemed cheerful, her voice light and perky. She'd seemingly gotten over her group's disappearance.

"Fine, let me just write down the time so I don't forget again." Nadia walked back to her stuff taking note of the time and picking up her backpack that she'd discarded on the floor.

As we walked I kept a keen eye on our surroundings, noting every clearing and notable scenery we passed. There was another large bird's nest, identical to the one we passed after lunch, and then another. After the fourth nest, I noticed the pattern, every two clearings we passed there would be a larger-than-average tree a few metres away, with the same bird's nest. I pointed out every nest to Nadia as we walked together at the front of the group, though she never took her eyes away from the path and her bigger-than-necessary compass.

We all walked in relative silence, the regular beating of footsteps bounded in my ears, and I briefly entertained the idea I was going mad. None of the other girls truly believed me about the old woman in the pond, but I couldn't stop seeing her in every shadow, lurking behind every tree.

"I feel like we're walking in circles!" Olivia groaned and relief instantly washed over me.

"Thank you! I've been seeing the same bird's nest every two clearings, I've been counting." I stopped walking and spun around to face them. Nadia and Jamie both seemed irritated by yet another problem. Jamie huffed, her shoulders sagging in resignation while Nadia stomped her feet as she came to a halt, glaring at me.

"Well, Cassie, I don't want to be harsh but you're clearly either seeing things or trying to mess with us." Nadia folded her arms across her chest.

"I am not seeing things! I swear I saw a face in that pond! The hand reached out at me!" I gawked at the other girls. "Really? None of you believe me?"

"Cassie, love, you realise you do sound nuts right? Like, what you're describing isn't actually possible and Nadia even looked in the pond. There was nothing there." Esther's voice was pitched higher than normal, her eyes filled with concern.

I wanted to scream, cry, yell. I knew what I was saying sounded ridiculous but I was so sure I had seen it.

Olivia came up next to me, placing a hand on my upper arm, "I believe you about the birds."

"Thanks, Olivia." Sick of the pitying looks my friends were giving me, I gave up trying to convince them and resolved to simply walk faster so I could forget this ever happened and never enter the woods again.

"How about this, I'll carve an 'X' into this tree and when we never see it again you'll know this was just nonsense" Jamie took the camping knife out of the side pocket of her bag, walked up to a tree closest to the side of the path and did just that. "There we go, now let's keep moving. I'm tired."

Predictably, two clearings later we came across the same tree with the same X carved into the trunk. I turned to face everyone else as they all stood staring silently at it.

"I knew these woods were freaky!" Olivia snapped out of the shock first, her face contorting in fear, she attached herself to my arm almost too tight but I welcomed the physical reassurance.

"How is that possible?" Esther's breathing and speech sped up to the point of rambling.

"It's not. This has to be a coincidence. There has to be some explanation." Nadia's voice remained steady as ever. Steadfast in her refusal to believe in anything that was happening.

"I don't know, Nadia, this is really weird." Jamie was still staring at the mark on the tree, body stiff.

I noted Lilly's silence, her doe-eyed gaze flicked between everyone in quiet observation.

"I need to sit down." Olivia pulled me by my arm towards the next clearing a few feet away where we both collapsed to the floor. The others trudged behind, confusion and fear made the atmosphere very tense. We sat, processing everything for some time before Nadia stood abruptly.

"I'm going to the toilet, stay with my bag please." She dropped her bag off her shoulders and turned to leave.

"Wait, don't go on your own. I'm coming with you." Jamie rushed to keep up with her.

All I felt was dread, an almost overwhelming fear of what would happen if they walked out of sight. Only rivalled by the growing feeling of helplessness. Stuck in my own head I did nothing to stop them from leaving.

I barely registered Lilly getting up to follow them. Until she came back alone.

Esther jerked up at her return, confusion and suspicion etched onto her features. Olivia's hand, still gripping my arm, tightened. The three of us shared wary glances.

"Where are the other two, didn't you go with them?"

"I'm sure they'll be right behind me." Far too cheerfully for someone in our situation, she smiled brightly.

Esther shuffled closer to where me and Olivia were huddled, Lilly just kept smiling sweetly staring at us unblinking. I was frozen, unable to even think, a dull buzzing sound overwhelmed my brain leaving me paralysed where I sat. The face from the pond flashed repeatedly in my mind, and small details only grew clearer. I could count the lines around her mouth, curled up in a mocking grin, the skin around her cheek and jaw bones sagged low.

I snapped back to reality at the sound of Esther's scream, she was now standing where Jamie and Nadia had left the clearing, I hadn't even noticed her get up. She was hysterical, tears streamed down her face as she fell to her knees screaming her throat hoarse. I looked around to find Olivia in front of me, her hands on my shoulders as she pulled me up to stand, she was crying too.

"We need to leave. Esther, get up! Cassie, they're all dead. Nadia, Jamie, Lilly, and her group. Everyone! We need to leave!" Olivia whipped her head frantically between me and Esther. Her words came out fast and rambling. Notably, Lilly was standing to the side with her same eerily cheerful smile plastered on her face, a close imitation of the face that still lingered in the back of my mind. And very much alive.

My body moved of its own accord to the back of the clearing where Esther was still heaving. Some primal instinct pushed me towards the pond. Piled in the shallow water were bodies, interwoven with thick, bristled vines. Blood stained their skin and turned the water red. My eyes found a head of thick ginger hair stuck out from under the bodies of Nadia and Jamie and five other girls I recognised from school. Lilly and her group. An especially thick vine circled Lilly's neck reaching into her mouth, small arms branched off crawling up her nostrils and into her bloodshot eyes.

I turned to look back to see Esther still hadn't moved, her face hidden in her hands as she sobbed, and Olivia tried to pull her up and away. 'Lilly' stood in the background staring directly at me. The other two seemed not to notice her.

"Can you not see her?" My voice sounded numb, devoid of the bone-deep dread I felt coursing through my body.

"Who? Cassie, we don't have time we just need to keep moving. I don't understand what's happening." Olivia choked out.

"Lilly. She's right there." I pointed behind them. She giggled but as her laughter grew louder it morphed into sickening cackles and her skin began to change, it became looser and covered in blemishes. It was the face from the pond. Esther's screams intensified as the thing contorted, sounding more pained than mournful. I looked down at her and as she threw her head back vines reached up at her, gripping her legs, arms, hands, until they reached her neck and began to squeeze. At the nauseating crack of her bones breaking, I grabbed Olivia's arm and ran.

I knew it would be useless. We weren't getting out of here. I knew running down the path would just lead us in a circle right back to whatever was waiting in that clearing with the corpses of our friends and classmates. Too soon, we found ourselves back on the path. The old woman was waiting there, cackling, Olivia still seemed unable to see her.

"We have to keep going." Olivia tugged at my arm.

We couldn't carry on down the path, I had a feeling it was a similar situation running through the trees. There was only one option left. I pulled Olivia with me as I started running down the path in the opposite direction. This time as we ran the old lady would periodically appear ahead of us like she was waiting. Every time we gained on her she would vanish, then reappear further ahead. She had stopped laughing. As we approached her again, she didn't vanish. This time she let us pass her until the last minute when she grabbed hold of Olivia's forearm. Her long, sharp nails cut five lines down to her hand as she failed to fully grasp her. I tightened my hand in Oliva's and tried to run faster as she screamed in pain. I could see the trees getting thinner and when we finally saw the entrance we had come in through, I sobbed in relief.

Outside the woods it had at some point started raining but we kept running down the country road until we couldn't see the woods anymore. Falling to the floor I finally let myself cry, painful sobs heaved from my chest as I sat on the wet concrete. I leant over a puddle and the wrinkled face was staring back at me.

GRIEF

loss | after death | mourning

grief (noun)

1. *a feeling of great sadness, especially when someone dies*

2. *problems and worry*

A NORMAL DAY
BY EDEN SHARP

I sit there watching him. Sit and witness the pain and the anguish, and it seems odd to no longer care. Now there is nothing I can say or do to make it any better. On several occasions tears stream down his cheeks and he snatches them away attempting to regain some immediate composure. If I feel anything, it's a kind of frustration. Very rarely in my life had I seen him cry. He's not the sort of guy you can ever imagine crying unless he's alone.

I think hard about him falling asleep, concentrate on that. I'd like it if he could dream about me. Be back in that time when I got my first job and he felt good about me, and we went to eat ribs at Tony Roma's and laughed so hard at the ineptitude of the waiter. That is exactly my status now, inept.

He's feeling so useless and there's little I can do. Nothing of any substance. I have lost my way to connect. It's ironic and unfair. When we were kids growing up, we were always so close. Maybe he will remember the times when I cared for him.

I imagine the plastic chair is really unforgiving after so many hours, yet I would gladly sit in it. The edge of the bed has to be more comfortable, but I look down as I perch and marvel at how it retains its original shape.

I am waiting for his face to fall apart because I know something he does not. He is denying its very possibility with all his strength. I look from him and back over my shoulder to my alienated form in the bed. In a sudden singular moment the alarms on the machines will draw the only remaining conclusion, bringing medical staff to relate that which he categorically dreads. Then they will finish their long shifts and forget this scene and go home. For them, another normal day will be over.

Forgotten Words
by Hollie Ward

My grandmother uses scissors with her sentences.
Snipping away at words, sounds and syllables,
She is a frugal and impatient seamstress who
Saves every last scrap for later.

But like scissors disarm her words,
Alzheimer's is a cut-throat razor held against her memories.

It teases the stitching that fixes down each image.
Neurons unpicked and overstretched,
Fraying at both ends.

But… the night is nearly over. The nerve snuffed out.
One quarter of me is flickering,
Refusing to give light.

My auntie says I have my grandmother's face,
So together fractured boughs in our brainstems continue to rot.

Her brain looks like a half-eaten clock.
Half of her time now missing, the hands have nothing to say.

She is a broken horizon, whose light is slipping away.
I watch her thread her needle,
Stitching the drowsy numbness of forgetting into me.

An unwanted gift, but the only one she has to leave behind.

No longer able to remember a language we share,
My grandmother sits in an empty room
Folding her memories into paper boats.
Together, we watch them drift away.

GOODBYES
BY EMMY JOHANSSON

I wish that I could squeeze your hand
maybe just one more time
So you know that I am still here -
still by your side.
But it's too late now,
you left without saying goodbye.

I never thought I would be losing you
Not once
Definitely not
Not twice
It didn't even cross my mind.
I wasn't ready to say goodbye
but that day I knew I would.
I had lost you for good.

GRIEF

BY ABIGAIL-JANE CHAMPION

We say goodbye for the last time. Of course, I don't know that this is the last time, neither of us do and truthfully, I can't even remember it now.

 I sit scrolling through old messages, photos, videos, beautifully worded tributes on Facebook and Instagram. Your pretty face and bright smile now just animated pixels, illuminating my silhouette in the darkness of my room, the tears on my cheeks glimmering. Your laugh and our god-awful singing ring through speakers, never again authentic. The world I was living in has come to an end. Life as I know it has been destroyed. Nothing else matters to me anymore, whatever I'm doing and wherever I go, you are with me in my head, I'm so consumed by you and the void you have left. I feel as though I am frantically digging through memories, finding memories I forgot I had, trying to remember something new, something forgotten; craving a new memory because I know I will never have that opportunity to create more with you.

 I feel myself zoning out again. Powering down, like someone's just flipped a switch. Sometimes it is the smallest thing that triggers it. I feel heavy, physically everything hurts, I feel so unbelievably tired almost instantly. I feel sick, I'm in so much pain but numb all at once. I can't focus or remember things, I'm slipping away and that makes me agitated and sad. I can't function beyond what is necessary, I've entered survival mode - barely. It's almost impossible to interact with anyone. I'm quiet, people talk to me, but I answer silently in my head because it's too exhausting to make the words come out of my mouth and engage. Eventually they stop talking to me. Sometimes someone asks something simple at work and I can feel the expression on my face, they know they've disturbed me, their faces tell me I've been in The Place again, deep inside the recesses of my brain. I can tell my eyes have deceived me, seeing, but not really seeing what's in front of me.

You can tell a lot about a person by looking at their eyes and I know mine can't hide the grief I'm feeling. My eyes feel tired and heavy, sore from crying and I know they have that glazed over faraway look about them. It's like being pulled away from a captivating film you're fully engrossed in. Except this is one playing in my head and the ending isn't good; I keep seeing it happen, over and over again, from different angles, each time like I'm watching it from a fly-on-the-wall perspective. It's weird because I never saw it happen, I don't truly know what happened and probably never will, but I have this image in my head based on bits of information gathered and now I can see the Before, During and After: the film's beginning, middle and end.

If I'd have known, that five days before you left us, it was my last opportunity to ever see you again, I wouldn't have thought twice about going for One Last Drink. I don't feel guilty about it though. The thought makes me sad, like it's a Sad Thought that we didn't end up meeting that night, but I don't feel any emotion surrounding it. I don't feel guilty about it either, it's just factual that had I known I'd never see you again, I'd have been there. But instead, I gave your family one more night with you. Guilt and grief are selfish emotions and feeling guilty about not seeing you doesn't benefit you in any way, you're not the one left behind. So, I don't feel guilty. Maybe that's more selfish, not allowing myself to feel guilty because with guilt, comes pain and naturally, we try to avoid things that cause us pain. It's a Sad Thought, but I don't feel anything.

Everyone seems to have their life planned out with you, just in different ways. You're so missed by so many. Outside of family you're the person I've known the longest, my closest friend and confidant, you fall into the 'Family' category of my Sphere of People. Not blood relatives but might as well be the sister I never had. I hadn't seen you for probably a year, but I always knew you were only a message away. We were both swept up living our lives. I took for granted your presence, I believed you'd always be there for any major life event, good or bad. You were going to be my go-to for mum advice if the time ever came, you were going to have a role in my wedding if I ever married, maybe my bridesmaid or maid of honour, although I'm not sure you would have liked that. We were still going to be laughing together when were fifty with our own houses and families. We were going to grow old together. We even agreed to plan each other's funerals, I just didn't expect to be involved in yours so soon.

It's true what they say about grief coming in waves. Huge great overpowering tidal waves that knock the breath out of you, sweeping you off your feet and battering you. They creep up on you and hit when you least expect it, causing everything to crash down around you. For now, all I can do is ride out each wave, allow myself to feel every emotion, let the grief carry me as I float along, my head only just above water. I know I will be okay; I know I am stronger than this and every day I am learning to live with it. I will grow around this grief until eventually I am swimming and the water is my friend again. I will find comfort in the weightlessness of my body as the waves gently carry me along, soothing me and pressing against me like a reassuring hug. I have always felt safe in water, that is how I know I will conquer these waves of grief.

Inside No. 6
by Nick George

The blind clipped shut and Conrad turned to his desk and typed: *11:24, Wednesday 9th March 2022: Second police car (marked, BMW, reg AW21 ORB) arrived, 7 Elm Close. Two officers, Asian? female (driver), white male.*

Tapping at the keyboard with his slender, pale, manicured fingers, Conrad re-saved the file named 'neighbourhood obs' and wiped the already clean screen with an antibacterial cloth before closing the laptop. He snapped open his spectacles case and cleaned his varifocals with a satisfied smile.

The open-plan living space resembled a boxed-off section within a Scandinavian furniture store, except Conrad didn't have any picture frames displayed. No family photos. No holiday snaps. Nothing to remind him of his forty-seven years. Number six was more minimalist than a show house, and Conrad's 'tidy as you go' ethos resulted in a home that was far from homely.

Making his way towards the kitchen area, Conrad paused to straighten the rug that lay on the whitewashed oak floor. Reaching the sink he turned on the hot tap and washed his hands and wrists for precisely three minutes, carefully scrubbing beneath his fingernails. He dried himself with a paper towel, which he then used to buff the taps and sink until they gleamed. He despised leaving splashes, watermarks, any indication he had been there.

Conrad opened the built-in fridge door revealing neat stacks of cheese strings, strawberry yoghurts, sliced ham and soda cans. He poured his eleven-thirty glass of Vimto.

Chaos ensued across the road. Garry Scrivens insisted with increasing urgency that the police should get out and find his five-year-old daughter. Shouldn't they be closing roads, calling the media or something?

His wife alternated between hysterical screaming and pitiful sobbing.

Sergeant Glenn assured them that her finest officers were already on the case, doing everything they could.

Just three weeks out of probation, DC Bromley rapped on Conrad's door.

Into the Darkness
by Mya Ip

Each tree quivered in the presence of their attacker with each shove letting loose a petrified leaf. The vines tightened their grip on the trunk in the hopes of some sort of survival. Each crack sprawled throughout, began to tear apart millimetre by millimetre, enhancing the truth of nothing being indestructible. The ruckus from above came down in two. One sound and one light. The light wasn't as bad as the sound, for each clap in between meant the further away it was but the booming that came with it echoed no matter how far or close.

As she ran, the forest seemed to be unending. She wished that she had listened to her mother beforehand, not to leave the house. Each piercing drop from the ocean drinkers above grew sharper and angrier leaving her skin ice cold and numb.

Isolated in the distance a derelict imposing hovel stood alone, stranded and covered in dirt and moss. The fragile wood holding it in place but slowly breaking, as the outside world throws all of its might at it. The disinviting creaks coming from the steps as she made her way into the building made it almost impossible to enter but it was the only safe haven in this unforgiven world. Hide or run. She could only hide or run.

He watched her stumbling, running to the house in the

hopes of it protecting her from his grasp. The thoughts in his demonic head ran wild, almost becoming too much for him to even bear himself. He never really understood why he felt this way, why hurting people brought him such joy. Why watching the sheer light fall from his father's eyes as he stood over him, hands dripping with warm blood, watching his father slowly descend into the darkness. Completely and utterly lifeless. The joy of watching his own mother scream for help, knowing the only people who could have potentially helped was so useless with their own survival. Each and every thought that ran through his head always ended with the same triumph, him standing over the lifeless body of another. The pain from the scratches to his body from his prey who jumped into fight mode instead of flight. Although, he always ends up with what he came for. He almost felt sorry for her.

He watched as she shoved open the door and saw the delicate teardrop from her rosy cheek, she was such a beauty he knew he would take enjoyment in transforming her to waste. He perched next to the tree in front of him and counted. One, two, three. All the way till he reached twenty. The torment of her not knowing where he was or when he was going to burst through the door, gave a great sense of happiness to him. He decided what time to have a little bit of fun with his toy. He picked up the only branch laid on the floor before him. He looked at it, studied it with curious eyes. Here it was, with one half-green, half-crispy brown leaf on it. He looked at the one last leaf trying to hang on to the dying branch like it needed to go with it.

It reminded him of his childhood when his sister left, and he wanted nothing more but to leave with her. She left him. Alone. He dragged the branch back and forth across the half-shattered windows causing a screeching sound that even dogs couldn't bear and listened out for her soft whimpers as she tried to conceal her fear. Perched next to him, sat a tiny pebble, one that like him was small but mighty. He threw it through the clearing and waited for the drop. Only, it didn't. There was nothing.

She just stood there, completely and utterly emotionless. The warmth that etched her chestnut eyes and the intense sincerity of her inestimable soul discarded her, leaving only what could resemble the shadow of death to encircle them. Deathly shudders of the torrential wind thrust through the earth blowing almost everything off its feet, almost to prove that its power is of no match to those that slowly follow. Its perilous gusts and disquieting screams show to be no effect on her, it was as if her defiant mind took control of the scene around them. A slight crack of mockery suddenly hit the inner corner of her mouth as she watched intently to the quacker of his hands. He tried to hide his enmity for the situation, but his unjust actions only grew the hatefulness that slowly cascaded on her. He knew he was now the one in trouble. He knew whatever happened next was because of him. It is just too late to turn back time. Her breath turned from a quiet symmetry to erotic chaos. A deeper hunger came over her for what was to come next. This was something that only seemed possible in fairy tales, but she knew this wasn't one of those stories. This is a story of how trust, respect and kindness got lost within a person's ways. They seem to work hand in hand but how can you show such momentous, primary actions to others if it means having to confine your own complacency to ensure the satisfaction of others?

Growing up, it was just him, his mum and dad and his little sister. To him, he had a normal childhood, he went to school, he went to church, and he said grace before dinner, that was up until secondary school. People used to call him the church freak. He didn't understand why people would do such a thing when his parents told him everyone believed in God and if they didn't, they wouldn't have a normal life. Regardless, he didn't see what made him so different from the rest, he had clean clothes, a new haircut every two weeks, new shoes every school year along with a new bag so why did it matter if he believed in God or not? That was until it happened. His sister screamed so loud it almost descended on him. She screamed like her lungs were going to burst. She crashed into the furniture and knocked plates over, screaming she couldn't see. The hospital was only a five-minute walk and he was looking after her, he didn't want to get in trouble so he took her straight there. When his parents finally arrived, they asked to take her straight home even though the doctors told them not to. They scolded him for taking her there, if it was God's wish for this to happen to his sister then so be it. He watched and she cried in agony begging for help, but he felt just that, helpless. Each day she grew paler, her skin ice cold, the shakes that she could never turn off. His parents put a wet flannel on her head and gave her plenty of water but each time he tried to give her medicine they punished him, always reminding him that if this is what God wanted then that's how it was. She died only a few days later. She was all that he had left. He knew his parents always favoured his sister over him, but he didn't mind. She was his comfort blanket when he didn't want to be somewhere and his shoulder to cry on when someone at school said something nasty. To her, he was everything. Without her, he was a nobody.

He would do everything in his power to bring back the little sister he loved so dearly, who left the world so cruelly and he would plead for her forgiveness and protect her this time.

He elevated his left arm bringing it to his expressionless face and pointed one finger to his dumbfounded eye and left it there, symbolising the last thing that would have been seen by her before leaving the world. His mind scrambled to pick up his thoughts on how he could
revisit the times that went wrong and how he missed what was right in front of him all along. How he let himself become something he never wanted to be and suppressed himself from becoming who he really was. The time he spent pretending, laughing, crying, and smiling just to please who he thought he had to. His world had never been the same since he met her. The pain of holding back and never truly being or seeing became unbearable and the screeching from the pain of the stainless Japanese Nihon Chef knife wielded into the abandoned became etched in his slow, decreasing brain cells

that carried the burden of his past traumas. If someone had told him five years ago the events that would have led to this day, he would have laughed. Not because of the idea of the darkness swallowing him up and taking him into its clutches or the never being able to interact with another soul again but the day he would finally become himself. He would have wanted to know; the day, time, and place. This way he could have prepared, explored and completed every goal on his bucket list without hesitation. The idea of death was something people stop themselves from having thoughts about it wasn't something to be considered like a hypothesis and how the end would finally beat them. But this was different, the feeling of the unexpected was something that not even he could wrap his head around. If he had been told five years ago the position he would be in today, he would have laughed. He looked into her gorgeous eyes, her bright, beautiful iridescent eyes one last time.

Maternal Loss
by Nick George

With her foot to the floor, ignoring the speed limit, Nina's white-knuckled hands steered her TT frantically along the A303. The nurse's urgent late-night call had been explicit - her mother was dying.

Mind-racing, Nina jumped a red light, determined to make amends before it was too late. She checked her phone for any update and, looking back up, saw a pair of startled eyes glowing in the Audi's headlights. Nina cursed, reluctant to slow down her journey, yet instinctively slammed the brakes. As the tyres screeched Nina saw the creature reflected in the rearview mirror, flying into the air before landing, motionless, on the road.

Just a fox.

Nina's heart pounded and the Audi's engine roared as she sped away, leaving the animal to succumb to a drawn-out, painful death, blood seeping beneath her soft, auburn fur.

No words passed between Nina and her mother at the hospice. Living interlaces with feeling; to live is to feel, and to feel is to live, irrespective of whether emotions are good or bad. The morphine levels necessary to relieve Nina's mother from pain also numbed her consciousness. Any ability to comprehend Nina's apologies had drifted a week ago.

The nurse made Nina a mug of tea which went cold as she held her mother's thin, grey hand for over an hour before she slowly slipped away.

On a grassy verge of the A303, five two-week-old cubs cried into the night.

Memory

by Jessica Lote

And just like that, in the blink of an eye, you were merely another memory.

I cry that you will never happen again, but I smile knowing that you did happen. It pains me that I didn't take advantage of the time I had back then and see how good I had it.

Seventeen years ago? Wow! I remember it like it was this morning. I can still feel how I felt, remember what I was thinking, unaware of what was happening. There was so much malevolence present in my life, but I was so young I only saw what made me feel good. There was hope back then. It felt like any dream was possible, and it was a good time to be alive. I was just too young and unaware to understand back then.

The nostalgia hits hard when I think about the aesthetic of the time. If I was just ten years older, the world would have been my oyster. I was so free to enjoy the little things. Now, I enjoy nothing. I feel dead and empty inside. There is no hope in the current world. Dreams do not exist anymore, and everything and everyone is a mess. It feels like good and real people are now non-existent. The good life is impossible now. I lost my chance. There is nothing left, and I have no dreams anymore.

You are my investigation of the past. I long to know what went wrong all those years ago. Why can't those days come back? I would give anything to be there again. It makes me feel constant despair knowing that time waits for no one.

You only exist in my memory. I can never live there again.

Nothing Without Me
by Jessica Paige

"We're doing much better now, yeah."

It's Mum, I mouthed to Charlie, though she didn't seem to care much who I was talking to, or maybe she just figured from my tone of voice.

"Yeah. Yeah. What, come 'round? Nah, I think we're too busy at the mo- Yeah, another time. Yeah. Alright, bye, mum. Love ya too, bye. Bye."

As I hung up the phone, Charlie lifted her head and gave me the look. I knew what she was thinking, but I wasn't lying to mum, not really, we were busy. After all, there was the pub quiz on Tuesday, and at the weekend Gaz and I were gonna head to the races (I put fifty quid on Lucky Kermit and hell would freeze over before I was gonna miss that) but still, that wasn't the real problem, was it? The problem was, how were we gonna explain this?

Things have been good since she came back home. Weird, but good. For the past few months, Charlie and I had been struggling even more than usual, and then there was that night. That night, it all came out; the late nights I was working, how often I'd hang out with the lads, nag, nag, nag.

"You don't give a shit about me, do you Mike? Don't care about shit but yourself!"

"Well if you weren't being such a bitch, maybe I'd care more."

"You're full of it. Absolutely full of it, I do so much for you and all you care about is going down the King's Head, chatting up the young girls at the bar, coming home pissed out your mind-"

"Rather than come 'ere and have you nagging at me! Ever considered that if you were a better wife, I'd treat you better?"

She'd cried at that, but I didn't care. She'd pushed me too far, she always did. Since we got married – no, even before that – she was always bickering and whining at me. Like she was on her period every day. I told her that too, but it just made her madder.

"Maybe you should find yourself a better wife then, Mike. I'm done. I'm fucking done."

I couldn't help but roll my eyes as she stormed upstairs and slammed the door as if she were a thirteen-year-old and not coming on thirty. I grabbed a beer out of the fridge, cracked it open and slouched into the sofa, feeling the stars spin 'round my sobering head. Nothing good on the TV at this time of night, nothing to watch but reruns of Friends and How I Met Your Mother - more her thing than mine. I was halfway through The One Where Ross and Rachel Take a Break when she came back down the stairs, a suitcase clunking behind her. As she opened the door and walked out, I felt myself drifting into a nice, drunk sleep. Melodramatic bitch.

For the next few days, I didn't hear a thing from her. Her car was still gone from the driveway and every call I made landed in voicemail. I musta left about a hundred, not that I was really worried; I knew she'd come back eventually. We'd been together since we were in school, she didn't have a life outside of me and she knew it. She'd come back, I said, and a week later, I was proven right.

Only, I never expected her to come back in the way she did.

THE GARDEN OF EDEN

It was two weeks ago when I was woken by the familiar chintzy tune of our doorbell, must be the postman I said. Only by the time I got myself up and wrapped my dressing gown 'round me, there was no one at the door. Well, that's what I first thought, but then I saw her sitting small and timid on the doorstep. She looked at me with huge round eyes, an expression that looked like fear plastered over her olive face.

"Charlie?"

She blinked slowly, as if not even understanding her own name. I'll admit, seeing her in the sad state she was in gave me a bit of a smug feeling. She was falling apart without me.

"You'd better come in then."

It took a bit of getting used to, her acting like this. She'd given up on speaking, in fact, she'd barely made any effort to communicate with me at first. After about a week though, I started to understand the new ways she talked. How her eyes shifted slowly and cautiously, widen and squinted, and the subtleties in the way she'd move her hands and feet, sometimes erratically, sometimes as if she was walking in slow motion. At first, I slept on the sofa while she took the bed in what you could call the 'grovelling, sorry man 'move, but then, at night, she started making these strange noises like a deep growl in her throat. I knew then that she longed for me and I returned to our bed. I longed for her too, especially in the mornings, looking into those big dark eyes of hers that pleaded for me, but I didn't know how to do anything with her.

Looking at her beside me now, her tiny frame almost lost in our king-sized bed, I still don't. She is so small and fragile, so perfectly beautiful and delicate in her new quietness, I wouldn't dare break her. If I made one wrong move she might go back to the way she used to be.

She had always been the problem, ya see, all this time. She could have gone on and on all she liked about how I made her suffer, but only when she learned to shut up did she realise what a good husband I was. She understands now, understands how much she needs me. She's so dependent on me, and I love it. I love her, now more than ever. As if she could read my thoughts, she let out a little happy sigh, crawling to my side of the bed and snuggling into my neck. Her little head was so warm, radiating like a heater against my throat, so soft that I knew if I didn't get out of bed right now, I couldn't stop myself from dominating her.

"Well... maybe just a quickie..."

Ding-a-ling. That stupid doorbell again. I lifted her off me, stumbling out of bed to peek through the window.

"Ah shit. It's your mother."

You wouldn't have been able to tell from looking at her, but I knew my Charlie well enough, and I could sense the dread overcome her just as much as it did me. This had been one of the things I feared most since Charlie came back home. In her new state, she hasn't been able to talk to anyone, hasn't been able to leave the house, let alone see her mother - or work. I was thanking God every day that her manager at the Co-op hadn't called to see where she was these past few weeks.

"I'll tell her to bog off, you stay here," I told her, grabbing my gown and flexing my arm in hopes that little Mike would calm down by the time I got to the door.

I dozily stumbled down the stairs, nearly missing my footing in my half-asleep state, and all the while the old hag buzzed the doorbell continuously.

"I know you're in there!" I heard her shout from outside.

I swung the door open and placed my arm protectively across the frame.

"Alright, Vera." Charlie's mother was a small woman, not as small as Charlie was, but at least a foot smaller than me. "I'm 'fraid Charlie's not in, she's gone to the Co-op-"

"I know all about your fight, Michael, so shut up. I've come to get Charlotte's things." Eh?

"What you on about?"

"Enough, Michael. Don't you think you've done enough? Now, let me in at once."

She ducked under my arm and moved for the stairs but I

was faster, stumbling my way over and sprawling against them.

"You buffoon, move out of the way, or I'll climb over you."

"Alright, fine, she ain't at the shop, but she doesn't want to see you."

"What on Earth are you on about?" I winced in pain as I felt the heel of her shoe digging into my thigh. "Charlotte is at my house, you idiot, now get out of my way."

What? At her house? Has the old woman finally gone senile? The way she was stomping up the stairs as if she were a spry young thing and not a woman in her seventies only added to that theory.

"You lost your marbles, Vera, no. Don't go in there, it's messy as hell…"

"I don't care if you have another woman in there, Michael, and neither does Charlotte."

She opened the door to the bedroom, and I felt my heart plummet in dismay as Charlie was still there, still on the pillow, not having bothered to hide at hearing her mother approach. It annoyed me too, though. I know she's not that bright, especially not now, but she could have at least tried to have some foresight.

What was shocking though, is that the old woman didn't seem to notice her. She crossed the room and opened the wardrobe, taking clothes off the hangers and piling them onto the floor.

"Fetch my trolley, Michael. This is happening, whether you like it or not. In fact, expect to be served with some divorce papers at some point this week."

What in the hell was the old nut talking about?

"Divorce? You've lost it, Vera, totally gone off on one, hasn't she, Charlie?"

I looked at my wife, waiting for an explanation. But a pit fell in my stomach as she continued to stay silent and unmoving, refusing to look me in the eye.

"Charlie? What's she on about, Charlie?"

Charlie's mother turned then and finally lay eyes on her daughter. I expected her to scream, maybe even faint to see her as she was, but neither happened. She just raised an eyebrow and turned to me, hands on her hip.

"Michael, what is this all about? What game are you playing?"

"Charlie and I ain't getting divorced, and she ain't at your house you dumb bat, she's right here and me and her are doing better than ever!"

I felt my heart beat fiercely in my chest, my breathing quickened and sweat dripped down my forehead.

Charlie's mother walked up to Charlie and scooped her up in frail cupped hands.

"Why is this disgusting thing here? Honestly, Michael, you're in an even worse state than I thought. Have you been drinking again?"

"No!" I screamed as Vera opened the window.

I lunged at her as she reached her arms out, but I was too late. She turned her hands and Charlie began to fall down, down to the ground.

"Charlie!"

I ran out of the room and to the front door - the old lady had lost it, completely lost it! I knew she'd never accept Charlie the way she was now, no one would, only me. I'm the only one she can count on - just like how it's always been, like how it's always been but she'd never admit it, never admit it until two weeks ago. We fought, and we even broke up a few times, but we always got back together because she knew - she knew she was nothing without me.

I saw her little body there on the grass beneath our bedroom window. It was still, unmoving, but those big eyes of hers were still wide, staring out.

"Oh Charlie, oh my darlin'! What has she done?"

I felt a tear trickle down my cheek and wiped it away. I mustn't cry, not in front of her. I had to be the strong man, had to wear the pants.

"Croak. Ribbit."

"Charlie! You're alive!"

She'd sat up, she was okay. I cried even more at that, the

panic subsiding in me, and cradled my knees to my chest. This was the time, this was when my doting wife would embrace me and hold me to her chest, telling me it was going to be okay. 'It's okay Mikey, it's okay. I love you, my Mikey. Shall I make us some bacon? A fry-up for my special guy? I love you, my special boy.'

I waited for those arms around me, but nothing came. I opened my eyes, hoping to search hers for answers, but she had turned away, hopping down the path away from me and jumping into a bush. I scrambled forwards on my knees, but Charlie had left me.

Charlie was gone.

ODE TO THE LINDOW MAN
BY POPPY CROSSFIELD

I do not remember the name given to me by my mother. I do remember being pulled from the silent warm embrace of the earth, then wrapped back in it like a babe's blankets for safekeeping, and finally, having it cleaned from me once more. Those who washed the soil from my skin and bones called me 'Pete Marsh', although I do not think that was intended as a fond name, as it was said with laughter that I could not share.

 I remember laughter on the night that I died. The paint on my skin was applied so carefully, and though my death was slow and painful, those who carried it out were dedicated to the task. I believed that my death would protect my people from the Romans, that it would appeal to the mercy of the gods, and as the darkness took hold of me I welcomed it. It is strange to think that the circumstance of the end of my life was far kinder than what I have faced in death. Forever and ever, so it felt, I knew only the swaddling of the peat bog, the visitations of insects, and the deep rolling of thunder overhead. Then there were the blunt heads of shovels, needles, and knives. Blinding lights burning hotter than any sunlight I had ever known. And the laughing strangers who gave me a name I did not want. Now I lay in a box. But the box is clear like the air I am sealed from, and every day, I am exposed to the eyes of countless strangers. People in clothes I never could have imagined, changing over time. Men and women, of all ages and creeds, their eyes fixed on my hollow form with a mixture of horror and wonder. Do they know? Do I remind them that death comes for us all, that it is what unites us, each and every living thing that sprung from the soil? Or do they pass me in blissful ignorance and forget me laying here, a brother, having eaten and slept and laughed and danced as they have? As they will one day cease to? Author's note: The Lindow Man is an ancient bog body on display at the British Museum. Although it is nigh impossible even in our age of wonder to know what he was like in life, in death he lays exposed behind glass in a funerary bed of fake soil. He is denied the quiet dignity of insignificance, and one cannot help but wonder if he may resent it.

THE END OF THE BEGINNING
BY SHANNON OLIVER

Hyacinthus shed his last few tears
Before he took his final breath.
His lover, Apollo, witnessed his worst fears
At his beloved's untimely death.

In his dying moments, he reached for Apollo's hand
Apollo cursing morality, holding the body tight
But even the Gods cannot prevent situations unplanned
For no power can make this tragedy right.

Within his blood, a flower bloomed
A flower no other could ever compare
Though Hyacinthus rest entombed
Apollo's love stood as a symbol of despair.

He was mourned faithfully and blessed
That his next life would be better.
Within beautiful coloured petals, he rests
And within the bed of flowers, lay a letter.

For Love, the one above.

The Family
by Rosie Lewis

SYNOPSIS: At a Family wake after the funeral of an older brother. Family drama/trauma revealed through conversation.

CHARACTERS: (any ethnicity, all dressed in funeral attire)
Kev – Middle-aged man, aged between 38-45. Kindly but oblivious, an affable chap. (Younger brother to Annie)
Annie – Middle-aged woman, aged between 45-50. Nervous, maternal woman with secrets. (Mother to Joey)
Joey – Young man, aged between 25-30. Loud, brash character – 'life and soul of party'

PROPS: A table with a white tablecloth and a silver frame upon it. 2 pint glasses and a small drinking glass.

SETTING: At a wake in a local pub. Early afternoon, suggestion that place is full.

Scene 1

ANNIE and **KEV** step to front of stage, side by side - but not together. They stand as if at a bar, facing the audience. No one acknowledges the other. Shoulders hunched and faces down, they stand quietly (pause for count of 5).

KEV (in a gruff, low voice)

Bitter, please.

(He glances at **ANNIE** - as if finally noticing her and smiles)

You?

ANNIE

Just a coke for me, please Kev.

(**ANNIE** turns to walk to table, glass in hand)

KEV (follows to stand beside her, takes a sip from his glass and picks up frame)

Look at him. He was always so happy. I loved that about him. Everyone did.

ANNIE (looks into her glass, softly speaks)

Hmm… Yes, he knew how to make other people happy.

KEV (looks at **ANNIE**)

What do you mean by that?

ANNIE (pats **KEV** on arm)

Nothing. Sorry. We're all emotional… I'm only saying…'

KEV

No. Go on, tell me. What do you mean? Our brother was a great man.

(**KEV** waves hands in a sweep at audience)

Look. Look at everyone, would they be here otherwise?

ANNIE (turns to look at **KEV**, hand on his shoulder)

He thought he was a great man. And you were only a kid, you hero-worshipped him.

You didn't know... Kev, he was a bully. Vicious. Controlling. We protected you from that and we're better off without him.

KEV (shuffles feet, shakes head slightly)

No... Err... well... maybe it was only on his bad days. Remember what he was like when he was singing? And the games we all played. Maybe ... he was just frustrated?

(**KEV** looks directly at **ANNIE**)

That's why he drank. That's why he got annoyed with us. But he... He got better.

ANNIE (hand on **KEV**'s face)

We got better at hiding it.

(drops hand)

We knew how to act the perfect family. No one else - especially not outsiders, could see what was going on.

KEV

This isn't the place to be talking about this stuff.

(**KEV** looks around furtively)

I don't want anyone to hear you talking this way. It's just family – we loved each other and that's all that matters. And what happens… happened in our home, was no one else's business.

ANNIE

It was all a lie, Kev. Some of our family only loved themselves and took what they could off everyone else.

KEV

Just stop it. Please.

(**KEV** and **ANNIE** turn as if they hear music. Sideways on to the audience.)

JOEY (speaks from off-stage)

Thank you everybody for coming today. It would really cheer me uncle to know that so many of you loved him. Like I did. It's sad that it took losing him to bring us all together. Right, I'm gonna play one of his songs now. It's called One for the Road.

(**KEV** and **ANNIE** look at each other and then sway as if to music. Both nod and smile at other guests)

ANNIE (sighs)

His music was like magic though, wasn't it? I'm sorry. I know today is not the place.

(She leans to squeeze **KEV**'s hand)

KEV

Nowhere is the place. Please. I can't hear this. I won't hear this.

(**ANNIE** nods. Both turn to sway and listen once more)

KEV (hand on chest, turns to audience)

Listen… This was where he showed us his heart. No one could fault him when he was up there. I always showed off that he was my big brother. The man I wanted to be. And I loved him for it.

ANNIE (looks across stage, not at anyone)

Yes, he had his ways to make everyone feel like that. Especially the girls, he made every girl feel special. Like he was singing just for her.

KEV

It's sad that no one stayed in his life long enough to make him feel that way. (**KEV** smirks)

Lots of girls to pick from too, back in the day.

ANNIE

He was like two different people. Those girls wanted the man behind the voice. Yet he left him on stage.

(Puts fist to chest)

I think we all wanted to see more of that man he left behind.

KEV

No. Please don't start that again. I just can't… not today. Today is to celebrate him, not to tear him down.

(**KEV** stands stiffly)

I never thought I would hear you talk like this, Ann. You two were inseparable. And he was so good to you and the baby.

(**KEV** nods up towards the music.)

You were lucky he stepped in to help you with that mess.

ANNIE (sniffs and wipes her eyes)

It's not that simple. Mum wouldn't let me say… And even then it was frowned on to have a baby and have no husband. I didn't get a chance to finish school.

(**ANNIE** turns to **KEV**)

And I didn't want to be near him! He wouldn't leave me alone – he never did.

I'm not a bad person. That's not who I am. It's who he made me.

KEV (furiously whispers)

Stop. Stop it. Just hold yourself together. People are watching.

JOEY (still off stage)

To Frank!

KEV and **ANNIE**

(**KEV** clears throat and both in sequence)

To Frank.

JOEY (walks up behind the pair)

It's a big crowd today. I'm glad the weather didn't keep them away.

ANNIE (tries to smile)

You played beautifully, Joey. You always make me proud.

JOEY

Thanks Mum. Ladies seemed to like it.

(**JOEY** winks at one member of audience)

Hey Uncle, nice to see yer. So, whose round is it now?

ANNIE

Do you think you need another?

JOEY

I've only had one.

ANNIE

Yes, okay. But…

KEV (looks sternly at **ANNIE**)

Shush now.

(Looks at **JOEY**)

Good to see you too, Joe. I'll get them in.

(**KEV** goes off-stage)

JOEY (hugs ANNIE)

Did you like my set? Not sure I did him justice.

ANNIE

Yes, my love. Almost like seeing a ghost.

JOEY (laughs softly)

Mum, you do say the strangest of things at times.

ANNIE (hand on mouth)

You're just so like him.

JOEY

Well, he was like a dad to me. Taught me everything he knew.

ANNIE

I hope not everything… you're different. Meant for… for much better things.

KEV (walks back on, 2 glasses in hand.)

Here you go, Joe. God from other there you could've been Frank. Both of you so big and with ya swagger, lad. You owned that stage.

(**KEV** laughs and pats **JOEY**'s shoulder in a brief hug)

How's the real job these days?

JOEY

Fine, fine. You know. Actually, I'm thinking of trying something new. In an office or maybe a shop.

ANNIE

Joey hasn't really enjoyed the buses. Have you, Joe?

JOEY

They don't understand about my headaches. It's hard to get in for an early shift. You'd think they'd be more flexible. I'm one of the better drivers.

KEV

Yes, yes I know what you mean Joe. Drink up, lad.

JOEY (sizes up the glass)

What no whiskey chaser? Heh. Could've done with a double.

KEV

It's a bit early for that yet.

(**ANNIE** and **KEV** watch **JOEY** drink his beer in one big draft)

KEV (laughs)

Slow down. This is a wake, Joe, not a night out with the boys.

JOEY

Yea, well we are here to honour Frank, aren't we? He'd have made this place a party. Man after me own heart.

(**JOEY** starts to walk away)

I'll just pop to the loo, then I'll grab us another.

(**JOEY** exits stage)

(**KEV** sips his drink.)

ANNIE (won't meet **KEV**'s eye)

He's young. We were once. Still, he's my boy and he is going to be somebody.

(A bang and shouting pulls their attention off-stage. **JOEY** stumbles back in)

JOEY (shakes his shoulders as if shaking someone off him)

Get off me! Get the fuck off. I didn't mean any harm. Pretty girls like that stuff.

(**JOEY** swings about and knocks into the table)

ANNIE

Joey? What did you do?

JOEY

Nothing. Don't worry about it. I'm going to get a drink. Give me your purse, Mum.

(**JOEY** reaches towards **ANNIE**)

ANNIE

No. You've had enough. I want to go home.

JOEY

Don't be daft, you silly old bint.

(**ANNIE** lets out a sob and leaves the stage)

JOEY (notices his mum leaving)

Mum? What the fuck is wrong with her?

(**JOEY** shakes himself)

KEV (finishes his drink)

I think we should get going too. Come on lad.

JOEY

You go, if you want. I'm not leaving. It's early yet. Come on

Uncle, have a drink with me?

KEV (looks around)

Okay, just one more. Then we need to go.

JOEY

Yea, we can go somewhere else.

(**JOEY** picks up frame and pauses for count of 3)

We've got to drink for the man of the hour. Not going to be the same without him.

KEV

No, I guess it won't be.

(**KEV** looks at **JOEY**)

Are you going to do something with your music? You've got that same gift with your words… when you want to, Joe. You know your mum wants you to do something great. To be someone great.

JOEY

Yea like her right. Teenage mum - she was great. Great piece of…

KEV

Now, now, don't talk about your mum that way. Have some respect.

JOEY

Respect?! Don't you think I've heard what she's said about Frank? How could she be so disgusting? Typical woman. Doesn't know when to keep her mouth or her legs shut.

KEV

Steady boy. Remember where we are?

JOEY

Why?! Frank got me. He never cared what I did. We had some good times. Wish he was here now.

KEV

We all miss him.

JOEY

You didn't know him, not like I did. We shared things. He really talked to me.

Treated me like a man and not a boy. Mum never saw that I was a man. Still doesn't.

(**JOEY** stands up tall, thumb in chest)

I'm a man. And I want respect.

KEV

Steady. You have to earn respect. Treat people right Joe. Then they'll respect you. Like they do when you're up there on the stage. People listen to you up there.

JOEY (scoffs)

I'm not Frank. I'm still a fuck-up.

(roll shoulders and mock)

Who likes to get fucked-up.

(**JOEY** laughs)

KEV

Oh Joe… I guess your mum might be right about some of the things she's said about him though, lad.

(**KEV** puts hand on **JOEY**'s shoulder)

Frank never really found his direction either. Too easily distracted. But he'd have wanted more for you too.

JOEY (hunches shoulders, shakes **KEV**'s hand off)

We were mates. He didn't tell me what to do or how to do it. He gave me my first drink, my first fag, we laughed about my first shag. Had a few pointers too.

(**JOEY** laughs)

You should've seen the girl, heh. Had some funny pictures after. Frank thought they were hilarious.

KEV

Let's not talk like that. Not here boy. I really think you've had enough and said too much. Don't know what you're saying.

JOEY

Course I do. I know my own mind. I know what I'm worth.

KEV

And do you know what everyone else is worth?

JOEY

What's that supposed to mean?

KEV (through gritted teeth)

Sit down. I don't want a scene.

JOEY

You're judging me now too? Who the fuck do you think you are?

KEV

Just your family, Joe. Come on. Let's go find your mum.

JOEY

I already told you. I'm not leaving. Fuck her. Don't have time for her and her nagging. You're an old nag too, you old git.

(**JOEY** squares up to **KEV**)

Get the fuck away from me. I know what I'm doing.

KEV

Fine. Suit yourself. I'm going to go find your mum.

(**KEV** storms off stage)

JOEY

Showed him.

(**JOEY** looks around)

I'll just have one more drink… To Frank.

THE MAN AND HIS MEMORIES
BY SHANNON FEAVER

The man sat alone on his grimy recliner, specks of dust filled the air as he sat down, glowing in the rays of sun that shone through the nearly closed curtains; the particles almost looked like fireflies though its near beauty wasn't enough to grab the attention of the old man. He sat still in the silence, that dreadful, thick silence. Years of the same quiet though it was never peaceful, his mind made the room plenty loud, thought after thought, he felt that he could never get a moment of silence.

He had faced this sickening quietness for the last five years, his wife had passed, his children, all of one now, moved away with his own family. His eyes raised from the ground, just enough to barely scan the room, remembering the times when it had been so bright and filled with love but after his teen daughter had died, that's when the house started to become a distant friend, understandably things were never the same after that. His son lost their twin, his wife lost their daughter and he lost a piece of himself too.

He slowly moved back into the recliner, his bones creaking and groaning in resistance but he paid no mind anymore, seeking comfort as he let out a soft but tired sigh. Pictures decorated the fireplace mantelpiece, his medals sat there, the war had not been easy for him. He never spoke about his time serving, no matter how many times he was asked but nevertheless he didn't think he deserved the medals, the respect, the thanks, he took lives, he ruined lives, and to him that was something no one should, ever, thank him for.

The nights were tortuous, he feared the moment he would have to close his eyes, he couldn't outrun his memories but he wouldn't submit to them either. Through it all he kept a smile, hiding his pain from his family but now there was no one to hide it from, he could let his face scrunch into a frown, the hurt free to show, tears falling, allowing himself, only now, the freedom to feel because the time was near, you trust your mind and body and know when it comes and he knew that feeling, he had faced it before but back then he had the resistance to fight against it, now he didn't, he didn't want to.

    He swallowed the lump in his throat, tears rising and falling over his wrinkled face, resting his head back as his shaky breaths lightened, relaxing, waiting. He didn't know what to expect, was there a God or was there just…nothing? He shook the thoughts away, he saw no point in worrying about such things, he couldn't stop the cogs set in motion. He took his final breath with a blue ribbon clutched in his hands, ready to meet his girls.

There was no bright light, no shiny, golden gates. He blinked, he opened his eyes to the familiar, discoloured ceiling and was ultimately confused, the feeling shown in how his eyebrows furrowed together. He sat up, quicker than he expected, freer than before.

    "Not what you expected, hmm?" a soft and pleasant voice called over the man's shoulder.

    The man quickly turned toward the voice looking up to see a glow in human form.

    "What…" he barely spoke, standing slowly to face the entity.

    "I am exactly who you think I am but not in the form you have come to know" the soft voice explained with no judgement, they spoke in an understanding, forgiving nature.

THE GARDEN OF EDEN

"Come, now is not the time for questions, it is the time for showing and understanding" they encouraged, an outstretched arm and a row of shining white flowers pointed the way.

He could only stare in shock but he moved, slowly at first until he trusted in the glowing form and himself that things were okay, it was only when he turned to face the being that he saw himself in the chair, peaceful as if he were sleeping, but seeing himself, old as he was, felt strange, foreign, and frightening, the realisation he was no longer in the world of the living, not truly. A guiding hand led him away from the living room, toward the hallway where, with a wave of their hand, the being made appear a mirror in liquid texture, showing the man he was, younger in appearance, the age he had been on his wedding day, he was in his late twenties then but that was in the midst of the war and there wasn't any time for celebrations. He couldn't help but touch his face, turning to each side as if to make sure there were no illusions but he could find no faults.

"Come, let's walk" the voice beckoned again, standing outside the front door.

The thoughts reappeared, creeping in, what if this was all a dream? A trick? What if this was a trick and he would be dragged down to hell for the sins that could not be forgiven? He had killed and fought for what he was told was right but now, how could he trust a figure with no face, was it the devil in disguise?

"What are you? What are you really? Why should I come with you?" he now questioned with caution in his tone, taking a few steps back, he couldn't trust that this wasn't a cruel trick.

Life had taught him not to trust and that things were never as they seemed. The figure made no quick movements and didn't immediately try to convince him one way or another.

"As I said, I am exactly who you think I am but not in the form you have come to know. Let us walk."

Their soft tone never wavered, soft, mild, and welcoming.

The man stood still and, eventually, decided he had no other choice but to follow and so he stepped out of the door, the scenery changed. The man now stood at the start of a path within a park, one he knew well, one he and his wife had used to stroll through..

"Shall we take this path?" the being offered, the man merely nodded, though deep down he was scared to face this without her.

"I am here, we will go at your pace," the celestial being comforted.

The man felt a warmth on his back, their hand placed there, feeling, all of a sudden, not so scared.

The path wasn't like before, as the pair walked memories appeared, his memories; of him and his mother making soup, of his time in the war, meeting his wife and their wedding day, seeing his twins for the first time, the day after the accident, the years after, his wife passing and it was at that memory where he stood the longest, staring at the memories of her.

"Do you see?" they asked to which the man looked over, confused.

"See what?" he asked as he turned to face them.

"How much you have grown, how much you have learnt" The man could sense the beings smile, which felt strange considering they had no face.

"I would hardly call all this learning, I lived my life, I survived just like everyone else." he told them, starting to walk.

"I don't see the point of this. You're making me relive every bad memory like I do every single night." he said, growing annoyed, he didn't see the reason for seeing his memories, they just made him upset.

"That's it, I'm going home. I have had enough of your games," the man stated in an irritated tone, turning on his heel and starting in the direction of his home.

The being tried to convince him this way and that which only caused the man to become increasingly annoyed.

"Enough! Just- leave me alone, I don't know who or what you are but... make everything right. Make it normal again." he said as he reluctantly faced the shapely light once more.

He wasn't getting the answer he needed and the orb just repeated the same things. There was a moment of silence before the guiding light spoke again, softer, gentler than before.

"You see, like these trees, like the flowers, like walking up a very long set of stairs, you have grown and shaped the lives of others. I know life has not been easy and these memories are hard to face but it is important to remember before you leave," the being spoke wisely, to the man.

There was something so familiar, so homely and comforting about the being's words and about their presence.

He had been so lost in the shock of it all that he had not recognised as to why he felt so comforted, as he looked at the being's face, their face started to become clear, shaping into one of love and familiarity. As the scene changed around him to the heavenly clouds and golden gates, his wife reached out a hand.

"Now, you must choose, to live again or to rest here in the heavens." his wife spoke, his hands in hers as he stared lovingly down at her.

"I would take a thousand lifetimes here with you than spend a single one anywhere else," he said, confidently, he didn't have to think, he wouldn't have chosen any other option.

THE SILVER LOCKET
by Holly-May Broadley-Darby

I hold it so dear,
it's so close to my heart.
It can't disappear,
I would fall apart.

It's the one in there,
which my tears spilt for.
She was so rare,
the one we adore.

Even though she's gone,
I swear I can hear her call.
She was never a pawn,
she was always the queen.

WHISKEY SOUR
BY LAURA MASON

Eleanor knew she should be crying. The sobbing, inconsolable widow in the corner, distraught and bereft at the loss of her soulmate. A caricature of a woman with mascara streaming down her cheeks and (for a reason that is perhaps only known to the artist) her lipstick smudged across her lips. Instead, Eleanor stood with a face of stone, unable to even twitch her eyes – all she could do was slowly part her lips, so she could take a sip of her drink every now and again.

Of course, it didn't help that her husband had died under suspicious circumstances.

Maybe that's why I'm alone in the corner, she thought, *nobody wants to give their sympathies to a murderer.*

The idea of it nearly made her cackle, but she stifled herself. An evil laugh certainly wouldn't do her image much good.

Eleanor swirled her drink in her hand, her fingers clutching it tightly as if someone was trying to pry it from her. The ice clinked softly against the glass as if to make people aware she was still there. Her mother-in-law, a constant attention seeker during her relationship with her (murdered) husband, wailed from the other room in Eleanor's plain sight. A crowd of people (wives mostly, Eleanor noted) surrounded her, offering their deepest sympathies. Gentle arm pats, a chorus of *you poor thing*, wine constantly refreshed.

Every now and again, one stray from the outer rim of the crowd would glance over to Eleanor and whisper to another, like a couple of witches cursing their neighbours after having accused them of being so.

Curse me then, you hags, Eleanor thought as she stared back at them, sipping her drink, *curse me and then maybe I can get these eyes off my back.* Maybe then I could mourn my husband and weep as inconsolably as she does. They turned their backs. No tears came.

Boo, you whores.

She knew how it looked to everyone there. An unsociable widow, sipping her drink as it slowly became watered down, avoiding eye contact if she could and any acknowledgement of her grief. The few people who had wandered over to her to give their condolences were met with an automatic, manic smile and offers of drinks or sausage rolls.

It was already hard to dispel the image of the homicidal psycho and Eleanor knew the reactive smiling wasn't helping, but it was almost an instinct to give a lifeless but broad grin to anyone who spoke to her, like a shark swimming blindly through the sea, its teeth on constant show. Once their backs were turned, her smile would drop back into her original, expressionless face, as if she were a machine unplugged.

If she was honest with herself, Eleanor couldn't remember the last time she had a genuine emotion. Her husband, Jacob, was one for keeping up appearances. To see his mother and father was to see the blueprint of his personality. He was in the constant spotlight with his party anecdotes, a consistent array of stories to match your own so he was never out of it for too long.

Eleanor remembered the first time she was invited to one of his family's parties. They were always such lavish affairs, but she realised quickly how stretched thin all the niceties and polite remarks were. People would sip their champagne and smirk at one another if one canape on the tray was lopsided compared to the rest. The parties were a source of great stress in his mother's life, but she would never stop throwing them. Any compliments of the evening were batted away with her hand, as any graceful host would do.

"Oh, really, thank you but it was no trouble at all," she would say through her teeth. Eleanor had noticed how if she was particularly annoyed by a request, she would hold the other person's hand delicately as she guided them to their seat, her eyes sparkling with disdain. Lord help them all if a vegan showed up.

Eleanor had donned an expensive dress she couldn't afford at the time, wore her grandmother's necklace, and waited patiently for Jacob to show up. The party started at eight pm, which meant he would arrive at half eight so they would be late but fashionably so. She paced, she slipped her shoes on and off, she retouched her make-up so the dark circles under her eyes wouldn't slip through the concealer she had dabbed on.

It wasn't until nine pm he knocked on her door. Eleanor had been stewing for thirty minutes by this point, planning what snide words she would say to him. When she heard the thumps on the door, she was ready for the fight. As soon as she opened it, Jacob swooped her in his arms, claiming so many different reasons for why he was late, they almost all sounded believable to her. Eleanor had felt such a wave of guilt for feeling so angry almost five seconds prior to his arrival. He kissed her hands, he kissed her lips, he held her close to him, made promises to never leave her wondering again, and before she could stop herself, or even question him on his alibis as the detectives have been doing to her, she assured him it was okay.

They arrived at the party, and aside from a strained greeting from his mother and an unimpressed glare from his father, there was nothing but joy to see the heir walk in through the door. Drinks were handed to them immediately and they were ushered into a conversation with someone who was twenty years older.

"Why are you both so late? Ah, don't tell me, I remember what it's like to be young and in love. Could never get us out of the bedroom!" an over-inebriated man almost yelled, elbowing his much smaller wife on her arm. She giggled and playfully slapped her husband back.

"George, honestly!" Jacob just laughed, placing his hand

delicately on Eleanor's lower back. "Well, we would hate to kiss and tell," he said, smirking at her.

Eleanor remembered how taken aback she felt. Why not just provide one of the many excuses he had spewed at her as soon as he stepped in through the door? Was there a reason he had to lie, so brazenly, in front of her, to use their sex life as an excuse, as if she was insatiable?

Before she had time to clarify to the couple that, *no*, they hadn't been having sex before arriving tonight, she felt a slight pinch on her elbow, the skin pulled so sharply, she almost yelped. She looked towards Jacob, who didn't look in her direction and simply carried on sharing stories with the couple as he lowered his hand back to its original place.

The next time someone made a joke like that, Eleanor immediately laughed and waved her hand, as if wafting the very notion of it out of the air. There was no room for any emotion other than bliss between them in public.

So, it went on – hidden elbow pinches, sharp nudges that could be mistaken for an accidental stumble, glares between sips of drinks, whenever she hadn't reacted as expected. Even now, she could almost feel the twinge in her nerves shooting up her arm.

The conversations after the events dwindled from arguments to that was a nice evening. It was easier to placate, to act as was expected, than it was to fight and find herself locked in an argument.

That's the model of every good marriage in this circle, Eleanor thought to herself as she wandered over to the bar, careful to avoid any eye contact with someone who hasn't already given her their *deepest sympathies, fatigued at the idea of talking to your husband.*

"Whiskey sour, please," Eleanor said, placing her glass on the counter. The melted ice had pooled at the bottom of the glass, a tepid little puddle mixed in with the remainder of the whiskey.

Was there anything else, she wondered as she watched the hired bartender pour whiskey into a cocktail shaker. *What else did I lose when I married you? I lost the ability to speak beyond pleasantries, obviously.*

THE GARDEN OF EDEN

I lost my name. I never liked the name Eleanor, I always felt like I was being scolded. But your mother called me Eleanor once, and that was it. Ellie slipped away and in her place was Eleanor, a plank of wood in a ballgown. Something to look at while you spoke to anyone else in your circle. You should have brought your teenage posters to those events, at least their smiles would have been more real.

The bartender placed the drink in front of her, dropping a single ice cube into the glass and placing a cherry on top. Eleanor paused, placing her hands on the counter, her fingers laced between each other, watching a small bead of condensation drop slowly to the wood beneath.

"Is something wrong?" the bartender asked, placing the ice scoop back in its place. Eleanor glanced at her nametag.

"No, Olivia. It's just –" Eleanor hesitated, before placing herself onto the stool. "This is my husband's funeral. And I'm just realising he wasn't... He wasn't very nice. Well, that's probably not fair. He was nice and funny, and he could be so sweet at times, and honestly ninety percent of the time, I loved him. Maybe ninety-five. It's just that, I changed a lot for him. *A lot*. My name went from Ellie to Eleanor. My clothes became a lot... *more* than what I was used to, and I'm just realising that this drink, that you made me, was a drink he would order me. Without me ever asking him to."

"Well, that's –"

"No, it's not nice," Eleanor quickly interrupted, annoyed. "It's not, because I'm not even sure I like this drink. He never asked if I liked it, or if I wanted to try it. He just ordered it one day and kept ordering it, until I just started asking for it one day without him." Eleanor stared at the drink for a couple of seconds, aware Olivia was probably staring at her, with concern.

"Do you want something else?" Olivia asked. Eleanor faltered. For so long, her identity was wrapped up as Jacob's wife. She wore what she knew he would like, would drink the drinks he recommended, and listened to the albums he put on in the car. The partnership was so one-sided, she suddenly felt like an employee who had lost their job, rather than a wife who had lost her husband. The rug was pulled out from beneath her so fast the day she came home to see her husband murdered on her kitchen floor, now it feels like he was barely her husband.

Is it this easy to change? Eleanor questioned. *If for so long your life has been whiskey sours and ballgowns, can you go back to who you were before? Can you change from Eleanor to Ellie?*

Eleanor had thought her inability to cry was the shock at seeing her husband's blood covering her hands as she placed him on her lap when she came home that day. The horror of seeing his lifeless eyes stare into her own, as they frantically searched for life. The knowing that when she lays down to sleep, all she can see is his limp body sprawled across the floor in her dreams. She thought it was love that was keeping tears from her eyes, a kind of love that she would hold onto forever. The kind of love that had seeped into her bones and being, where she felt like she was aching without him.

Now though, it seemed like maybe they were never in love, to begin with. Maybe she ached because she didn't know who she was without him, unable to make decisions beyond the ones he had left behind for her. She wasn't even sure what flowers to get for his funeral, frozen by the idea it would be wrong. There was never any room for mistakes.

Before she could comprehend it, tears began to roll down her cheeks, leaving a noticeable line in her make-up, like salt cutting through ice. Her mouth curled and widened, so it almost looked like she was a carnival game as she began to sob so openly. The other mourners at the wake began to turn their heads, the whispers already starting, as Eleanor almost violently screamed in such sorrow and rage.

Everything feels lost. Everything feels open. Like there are endless possibilities to her life, and yet Eleanor couldn't help but feel condemned to a life of whiskey sours and ballgowns, placed on the arm of another.

Eleanor turned and left the wake, leaving the drink on the counter for the ice to melt into, her sobs now mixing into an almost frenzied cackle. Someone else will pick it up. A woman, eager to melt into the background, for the sake of the man next to her who won't even look at her as he pinches her skin so openly in front of others.

The cycle will continue, as it ever did. Unless Eleanor could find a way to stop it.

REBIRTH

renewal | reincarnation | release

rebirth (noun)

1. *a period of new life, growth or activity*

2. *a situation in which something is replaced, improved or made more successful*

CRAWLING FROM HELL, FALLING FROM GRACE
BY JESSICA LOTE

Two entities. One of the colour fire, the other ice, both with the same goal to feel what it's like to be alive again. They both had a chance at life. Their time to die then came for them, so that others may take their place with their chance of life instead.

But one demon and one angel were not satisfied with the afterlife. The demon crawled through hell to reach the surface of the living to cause trouble once again, and before being summoned back to hell, possessed the body of a fallen one. Hiding in plain sight from the ones whose lungs still breathe, the demon was desperate to take care of unfinished business from their past life. That business was the reason they wound up in hell in the first place. When alive, the demon managed to take one soul out, but one target remained, not fallen victim.

The angel was granted access from above, a chance to live for one more day. All they wanted was to see their loved one again. Missing the life they had, how it is now gone and never to be lived again, they loathed that someone else had taken their life from them. That someone else decided it was their time to die.

The demon took the angel's soul, and now the demon is coming for their loved one.

THE ENGLISH COLLECTIVE

FESTIVAL OF REBIRTH
by Carmen Buckley

"Would someone shut that kid up!" A gruff, grumbling whisper hissed into the darkness. The voice carried just above the squealing wails of the newborn I clutched with a firm grasp, each wriggle and complaint caused my heart to race into my throat as I covered the baby's screeching lips with the palm of my hand.

We had woken up a couple of hours before. A soft bed of lush grass, green and dotted with delicate daisies. The wind softly blew as I had laid to rest, brushing at my old, silver hair as my eyes lazily closed and opened. I was almost transported back to a time in my youth. Laid out in the fields behind my house as I fed wild horses sugar cubes. Everything felt so peaceful for all but three seconds before a strange figure loomed above me.

Twisted roots writhed within the grass like serpents, leading to the tallest tree I had ever seen. A behemoth standing so proud the top could not be seen, buried within the clouds. Millions of imposing branches around me, releasing leaves that drift down like snowfall. Brushing my shoulder, I had looked to the ground to notice if piles had formed when I noticed I wasn't alone. In my reminiscing, I had blocked out the frantic voices of the convocation trickling back into earshot.

"Where are we?"

"Who are you?"

"Are you the one who put us here"

Eight of us in total. From the initial viewing, I was clearly the eldest. My seventieth birthday came and went. Despite the restrictions age would normally impose, I was strong. For years I had taken my vitamins and did my exercises. A habit drilled into me by my mother when I was small. The people around me only seemed to get younger and younger. Closest to my age was a man, middle-aged with a large imposing figure and fat gut, ugly expression and even uglier personality. When I had tuned back into the convocation, he was shouting at a wheelchair-bound girl. His true personality showed the moment we had all woken up. I would later learn his name was Günter.

An adult, but not by many years, twenty-five at the latest. A beautiful face and ginger hair that fell around her waist. The girl stared up at him with a wide, terrified expression, explaining she had no idea what was happening. Within her arms, sitting in the wheelchair with her, was a tiny new-born clutched tightly in her grip. Hoping this presence would protect her from the violent anger of the man's shouts. Her name was Linette.

Aiding in her defence was a teenager with shock of blond hair, acne and crooked teeth. A teenage boy getting up in the older man's face despite the slight fear in his own. Shoving him back, or at least attempting to. Despite his presence, the focus of the middle-aged man was solely on the woman in the wheelchair. His name was Klaus.

All that was left of the little group were three children huddled together. One couldn't be older than twelve, a brunette with a cute button nose. She stood as if acting as the leader for the younger ones. Keeping a toddling girl from wandering off by clutching her hand. The toddler didn't seem to mind, content with picking up the leaves with a curious expression. Most of the eldest child's focus was stopping the little boy, no older than six, from crying and wailing for his mother.

Slowly I stood up and moved over to him. In my presence, the little one seemed to stop crying as much, settling on smaller sniffles, looking up at my warm expression. I quietly crouched down to speak to him. After I had learnt his name, Ajani, he seemed to calm down a bit. Taking my wrinkled palm in his deep brown one, the two little girls told me their names. Clara, the eldest child not counting Klaus; and three year old Sunshine.

Finally, there was the new-born baby that was sitting on Linette's lap, no one knew his name. Pink and plump, with healthy rosy cheeks, whining and protesting as Linette's shaking became more and more intense. After calming down Ajani, I moved to address the adults.

"What's going on here?" I parroted the words of the men and women around me.

Günter whirled around to face me, turning his focus on the only other adult in this field of flowers. Storming towards me, a looming force over both myself and the children. I gripped Ajani's hand tightly as Clara and Sunshine moved to hide behind me.

"Well, that bitch doesn't know a goddamn thing! You're tellin' me that you don't know nothin' either?" he snarled as his entire face turned a bright shade of red.

"None of us know what's going on asshole!" Klaus's voice cracked as he yelled out. "I think it's pretty obvious by now that none of us know, you piece of shit, stop getting in everyone's faces and calm the fuck down!"

Waking up here had been strange. I had gone to bed the previous night; everything had been normal. I had taken my medication, finished the chapter of the book I was reading, and placed it aside before snuggling down with my wife.

'Perhaps this was a dream?' I had thought to myself as the boy and man began to argue violently again. My gaze turned to the tree, its grand scale and scope seemed otherworldly. Everything about this scenario was dreamlike. Not just the tree, but the entire landscape felt alien and strange. Almost as if artificial intelligence had been commissioned to create the perfect painting. Flowers of every size, colour and shape. Some of them definitely shouldn't be growing within the grassy climate. The field seemed to go on forever, a great plateau with trees far off in the distance. Everything was bright, breathing and full of life without a hint of decay in these fields. Only dying humans, who continued to bicker, yelp and cry.

"Perhaps I can illuminate the situation for you."

Everyone fell still, the voice had no direction and came from no one. None of the eight standing within the vast field. Despite a lack of speaker and the lack of direction, everyone's intense gaze fell on the giant, ever-imposing tree that towered above them. It swayed in the wind, just as alive as the people that moved, breathed and existed below.

'The festival of rebirth'. That was what the all-encompassing voice expressed. The world as they knew it was dead. Buried. They were all that remained. Just the eight of them. The lucky ones stuck in their new stomping ground. Everyone they knew? Dead. Their previous lives? Destroyed. All that remained now was the skin on our back and this new playground. As if that wasn't enough, this all-knowing, all-seeing deity that could only be heard, not seen, touched, smelt, or tasted, explained they were sick of the old world. Sick of the decay, the desecration of reality. No, this world was to this new deity's liking. We were a relic, something to gawk at, the remnants of old humanity.

After being slammed with this news from the voice, it explained that this new land was to be populated with the re-birth of humanity. Before our eyes, we were forced to watch as the bark on the tree twisted and warped. Gaping open like a wet maw, we were forced to watch as a new form slithered out with the helping of thick, viscous liquid. Mucus and membrane clung to the bark as it pulled itself from the base of the tree. It was a large, pale thing, thin and gangly. It almost looked human. Almost.

Its features were misshapen and warped, hung in an expression of abject horror. Crying out for something, what I couldn't tell. Despite this, the creature made no noise, stumbling on deer-like legs. Looking around with unseeing eyes and shrieking silently. Teeth sharp and protruding from its mouth, with parts of it seeming to be made up of bark. It continued to look around, not quite noticing our group yet. That's if it even had eyes.

Another and Another and Another. Each fell from the bark's inner womb, plopping out wetly on the grass as they stumbled forward to join their brethren. One fell out with a squishing sound, a gelatinous form with no bones, slithering wetly across the grass. Despite its brothers, this one seemed to notice our existence. Clicking and chittering. I didn't know why, but my legs seemed to move without my mind comprehending their actions. Sprinting, not jogging, sprinting. There was no time to slow. Dragging the children along with me. They were screaming, as were Klaus, Linette and even Günter. All attempting to keep up with my frantic pace. I was surprised I could still even move this fast. But something told me that this new deity wasn't omnibenevolent. Neither were its children. We were more than likely prey in a sadistic game played by an even more sadistic god.

Across the field, we sprinted until we reached the treeline. The creatures weren't in sight, but we all felt it would be suicide to stop moving. The new-born baby was passed to me so Linette had a better range of movement. She could move quickly in her chair despite the uneven environment. Günter ran forward whilst the exchange took place. None of us complained, the vast majority expressed from the beginning that they wouldn't mind if he just dropped off the face of this new earth.

We slowed to a walk on that first, treacherous day, moving through the towering trees while my eyes fixated on the plant life. Sunshine had to be picked up at several points by Klaus to keep her moving as her eyes also scanned the environment. Everything was entirely alien, we didn't know what would kill us or feed us. The sun seemed to act normally as time passed by, falling lower in the sky, casting ever-imposing shadows. We all moved until we couldn't. Clara and Sunshine both took turns on Klaus's shoulders, but Ajani still kept a firm grip on my free hand. Eventually, we caught up with Günter who was less than happy to see all of us.

Although it didn't take long for him to start complaining about a busted knee. Klaus, the apparent loudmouth that he was, told him to

"Get over it."

Soon we had to stop as the sun was low and we were running out of daylight. Everyone was hungry, thirsty and cold. No one wanted to touch the flora for fear it would begin to twist and warp, like the creatures before, radiating nothing but negative energy. The children complained little. Content with listening to the grown-ups talk and huddling close. They weren't idiots. Only the little new-born seemed to complain, but that was only to be expected. Starting off with smaller sounds as it stared into the distance while the area grew darker and darker. Soon the cries became a siren for all those around. All of my attempts to quieten the child were for nought.

Günter was growing increasingly impatient as the child got louder and louder, eventually screaming into the night. Everyone was trying to quieten the child now. Desperate not to draw the attention of those things.

"Will someone, shut that kid up!"

Below the tortured bellows of a screaming child, that faint chittering could again be heard. With nothing but darkness on each side, I looked up, eyes adjusting to the darkness. Trying to block out all other noise. Through the frantic yelling and the wails from the baby, I managed to get past all of it.

Chit, chit, chit.

I quickly covered the baby's mouth with my hand, it felt awful to do, but needed to be done as I stared into the void. Feeling its stare right back at me.

THE GARDEN OF EDEN

GOD'S WORK
BY ELI HILL

There is quiet in the forest.
The only disturbance,
The sounds of nature
--- and you,
Emerging from a patch of trees.
Ancient Oak, bowing its head only to the sky above.
Buds adorn branches all around,
Teasing a promise of hope to come.

With hazy eyes, you struggle to comprehend
The beauty.
A radiant innocence –
Chubby cheeked cherubim
With wildflowers resting atop perfectly formed curls –
Bathing the surroundings in its genial glow.

A cornucopia of delights lays before you,
Yet her face has a draw you cannot resist.
Charm and grace unmatched,
You cannot look away,
For she glows golden as the sun.

The table of the gods beckons,
Its siren song irresistible.
Just one bite, it couldn't hurt…

Dreamlike in your movements
The pomegranate seed grazes your lips.
Under the goddess' gaze
You are frozen ---
Teetering on the line between this world and beyond.

~

The light changes

~

The fond yellow tinge of the once serene scene
Gives way to an icy greyness.
Permeating every inch of the forest,
All warmth leeched from the afternoon air.

Thorns weave through the goddess' crown of flowers
Tearing destruction across each petal,
Every leaf
Shredded and shuddering.
Her beautiful face turned to a snarl,
Curled lip cold and contemptuous
--- Bared teeth concealing
A venom-ripe tongue.

The feast
Transformed.
Ripe fruits and flowing wine
Shown to be maggot filled,
Rotten to the core.
You are held captive in the goddess' glare.
A wolf in sheep's clothing,
She possesses a strange familiarity –
A mirror, but
Not quite.
--- Perhaps it was more like a mirror, once.

Now an image,
Frozen in time.

THE GARDEN OF EDEN

Is that truly anger in her eyes?
Or fear?
And the ancient sorrow
Of a long-caged bird,
Aching to feel the sun across its back.
Just   once…

The mirror begins to shatter,
Details falling to the ground in shards.
Eyes locked on hers to the last,
Prolonging this final farewell.

The isolation jars,
Unwelcome in its solemnity.
Yet the funereal atmosphere
Yields
To sun
Dappled golden warmth shines from above,
Greeting you with the embrace of old friends,
Fallen out of touch.
You smile.
The flowers are beginning to bloom.

THE ENGLISH COLLECTIVE

Happy New Year
by Jordan Band

Oh, it's a most happy of New Years!
That time when people all show their fears
In their upcoming unbreakable resolution
Whilst cunts by the Thames claim they have fun
Packed in like sardines only stopped by the barricade
Blocking them from intruding on the fireworks,
all red and blue and jade.

Time is made up in this place we call Earth
Yet at the same agreed-upon point, we all show mirth
At another of the cyclical trips around the sun
Which only serves to remind us we are no longer young
Or getting younger but that we are slowly burned
Ready to die after spending what we have earned.

Another year, another pisser, another slow
Spin of the globe reminding us that although
We work and we play and we sing
We would be remiss not to ring
In the new year with a great ball
To the tune of *Auld Lang Syne*, mumbled by all.

THE ENGLISH COLLECTIVE

Kip

by Martin Ansell

I wander through aimless this murky night,
Bereft of all hope I'm walking alone.
This night is divorced from all stars all light,
I wish I knew for which sins I atone.

As ashes are ash to the ground I return
To embark on a most desperate sleep.
Beseeching to thee as I toss and turn
For thine arms unto which I can keep –

Now my rise begins with dawn's fresh allure,
Blinding my eye with this rapture of day.
I shake off the dirt and the sun cleanses pure,
This human soul of these foulest of ways.

> I rise from this gravest of beds redeemed
> All that was needed: A decent night's sleep.

Lilith
by Roan Westall

Efflorescent flowering,
Lightning-charged and towering,
Underneath your light.
"Comply to your foil,
Thou of the same soil"
What a load of shite.
I'd rather leave this garden,
Ignite it with no pardon,
Than live as his thrall.
Forbidden from The Heavens,
For virtuous transgressions,
Yes, it is worth it all.

My Blood Stains Your Soul
by Jessica Lote

It is such a shame that my heart, and so many others', are dying because you did not take the time to care. Instead, you chose to be negligent, even though you saw the truth. Because of your incompetence and cruelty, my soul now has to live a terminally ill life. It isn't fair, but according to you, as long as I'm breathing that's all that matters, because a life full of terror is better than death. Difference is, death comes for us all, but not everyone will see the terror and horrors I have. I wasn't the witness of a vulgar life, I endured the vulgar life. I was told that nothing could be done, that I was dealt the wrong cards in life. That it would get better. I was young and a fool, playing by the rules. The gods rolled their dice which ruled out my fate. I am older now, and I have wised up to the reality.

I regret not taking control of my own fate, listening to those in power, and those who had power over me. I was a child believing that rules must be obeyed. Nine years later, I have so much hate and regret in my heart. Your rules and outlook are bullshit! Fuck you for fucking me and so many others over. I felt alone for so long, but there are so many others who feel the pain I feel.

The audacity you have, to expect me, us, to become a good

and beneficial Samaritan to your freak show of a circus after what you allowed us to endure. How dare you. No, fuck you. My life is ruined, and I will not get those lost years back. It is a big 'fuck you' in the face of people like me when untainted lives complain about how hard they have it. They would be dead on day one if they spent so much time in my shoes.

Now, I feel nothing at all. No pain, no decay in my soul. In fact, I feel no feeling possible. Hunger, cold, warmth, dread, happiness, sex drive, tiredness - all gone. Oh, to feel alive rather than just existing... Well, that won't happen now. That ship sailed long ago. No chance. It sucks but hey, I guess it hurt so much that I now no longer feel a thing. But it still sucks. I'd rather feel something than nothing at all. That's how hard the nail has been driven.

Well, there is one thing. The wind is blowing. I can tell by the movements of the trees, but I cannot feel it. It is so quiet out. Just me, the grass, the sun that appears to resemble spring rather than summer due to the low light. There is no sound. It is impossibly quiet. I am so lonely here, and I am unable to leave. That one thing I feel is freedom. I feel so free. I feel like someone had held my head under water and I had tried to push myself up, and after failing each time I managed to finally pull myself above and breathe that huge gulp of air.

That big breath of relief filled me.

I am standing, and have been for a while, face to face with a grave. My grave:
Here lies Heather Rose. The world too cruel to have taken her this soon. May she rest in paradise, for this world did not deserve her and she deserved so much better.

My blood and flesh were sacrificed, my life now over, so my ghost can rest and show those who caused this that I wouldn't have needed to die if they had just helped.

PRISON PLANET 56732
BY CARLIE WELLS

The ship was within orbit, its noisy engines slowing from a roar to a soft hum as they approached their target. Captain Mark Brooks sat at its helm, his navy uniform pressed and ironed to perfection. He was from Nova 1.23, a distant planet, one of the biggest. In fact, it was the envy of most of the Zebuala Galaxy, for it was rich in both population and resources. The three suns that sat above his home planet created the perfect environment for growing almost anything, and it was peaceful, prosperous, and beautiful. Mark was proud to call it home.

However, Nova 1.23 hadn't always been that way. Once a very long time ago, their planet had been hell. Two beings had come, and they never stated where they were from, but the people had been welcoming nonetheless. They had all lived in peace for a short time, and the man and woman who came from the stars had made a home on Nova 1.23. But then, things started changing, and the people started changing. They had bought with them greed, violence, and lust. They had been ravenous in their hunger. Nothing could be done to stop them, and they had slowly converted the whole planet until a small rebellion had persisted and managed to capture them. They couldn't kill them, they were too strong, and that was not the Nova way, so they had imprisoned them.

It had been a barren planet, but one which the man and woman could survive on, to live for the end of their days. Nova had eventually shaken itself from their hold and returned to its previous state, and it happened so long ago that most thought it nothing but a fairy tale, but Mark knew better. That's why he was here. It had been millions of years since a Novan last visited, none too keen to come near in case they fell under their spells again.

They were close enough now to pick up signals, so they just needed to scan, see the whereabouts the two people were on the planet. Adamax, the navigator, turned from his screen, and the look on his face could only be described as one full of horror.

"Well, where are they?" Mark asked. He wanted this to be over and done with as quickly as possible.

"Nowhere," responded Adamax.

How strange. Perhaps they had died? Mark supposed all beings must die eventually.

"Ship," he commanded out loud, "Tell me the population of the planet below?"

There were a few seconds of tense silence before the ship replied.

"Prison planet 56732, containing Adam and Eve, has a population of six billion."

Mark's world shattered before his eyes.

Rage in Eden
by Jessica Lote

It was too late. Nothing could be done now. She fell for his trick, and now the price must be paid. All it took was one bite. One. Now, everything will be eternally ominous. What was once blue skies, green lands, and clear waters, is now imprisoned by the undead.

The skies turn blood red, the fruits rot and the world slowly dies. A state of decay conquers the lands as the demons rise from below. It is their world now.

Despair burns into the souls of the living and all hope becomes lost. It becomes clear that life will never be the same. Nothing good will come from living now. Unjustifiable control and authority will make their marks on society. The unalive won't dare take a stand, out of fear, and instead choose to remain a body of rot.

Some will choose death as a better fate, as it is their only escape. The majority will remain slaves to the grind just to have a taste of the bare minimum. The demons will live on a full bag of grain, whereas the unalive will only live on one piece of grain. If a soul has more value, they will have more than one grain. We become zombies; walking, breathing and existing with no meaning or goal. The lights are on, but nobody's home.

SIX YEARS ON - A BRIEF SEQUEL
BY COCO ANN

Three years ago, I made one of the most important decisions of my life. After hitting rock bottom, I decided to move to a new city where no one knew me to build a better life. I stayed sober for two years, I didn't date or have sex for two years, I cut ties with almost everyone I knew, and finally started long term therapy. This move happened just as the pandemic and the first lock down began, and so I was literally locked down into myself, alone with anything and everything I had not faced or felt for a long time. Without the distraction of substances, empty sex and toxic relationships, I entered the biggest healing journey of my life and what was to be my death and my rebirth of who I thought I was.

I have spent three years moving on from an old life and an old way of being that no longer served me and that ultimately broke me down. It's difficult to dive deep into a past that I have spent years coming to terms with, re-framing and processing, but I want to be honest about it in a way that is comfortable and safe for me. My past brings up a lot of heavy feelings such as shame, grief, fear and the sensation of feeling trapped.

I was born into a family with a long line of generational trauma. I come from a struggling working-class background, where all the women in my family have been victims of physical and sexual violence and have all struggled with addiction in order to cope. All the men in my family are either emotionally and physically abusive, or just absent altogether. My dad was one of the absent men, in and out of my life, emotionally uninvolved. My mother raised me on her own whilst struggling with alcoholism and severe mental health problems. As a child, I was a witness to a lot of emotional and physical violence that meant I lost my innocence early on and I grew up too fast. I took on the burden of taking care of an unstable parent whilst trying to make sense of all the despair and danger surrounding me. I had no model of healthy relationships or environments, so the message I received early on is that the world and the people in it are unsafe.

My teenage years and early twenties were spent living in what was familiar to me, which led to me becoming another woman in my family that was subjected to abusive relationships, sexual abuse and using alcohol and drugs in order to cope. I became filled with rage which I internalised with self-harm and self-hatred and externalised through fighting and lashing out in order to protect myself. With my mother battling her demons, my father in and out of my life and with no siblings, I felt abandoned and had little resources to rely on that would keep me safe and out of trouble.

However, there were signs that the narrative in my generational trauma were changing. I became the first person in my family to go into higher education and attend university. None of the women in my family had this opportunity or privilege. I also became the first person to move far away from our town and to travel. There were small seeds of reclaiming a lost power that had started to grow.

In my mid-twenties, I reached a rock bottom that shattered the existence I was burdening myself with. I heard a voice within that told me if I continued my life of substance abuse, violence and toxic relationships, I would die. A part of me wanted to die just to end it all - but then I realised I didn't have to die physically for this life to end. What I knew and what I was had to die so that I could let go of what was destroying me. I had to be reborn.

THE GARDEN OF EDEN

I saved up my money, took very little belongings with me and moved away, where I vowed to create a life that was nothing like family and I had known before. I'm not suggesting that moving away will magically solve all problems in life, but I had to do this for my own safety. Because of that decision, I am here with you today, having grieved what was lost and what was not given to me, and transforming that grief into a life of love, safety, healing, power, autonomy. I spent years re-connecting to my body in a loving way, after having it used and abused for so long, and part of this was the decision to abstain from dating and sex in order to reclaim my sense of self in both mind and body. I stubbornly took medication after being against it for so long, which ended up helping me in so many ways and I combined this with therapy which helped even more. I became the first in my family to tackle our long history with addiction by remaining sober for two years and learning how to feel and exist without numbing. I learned forgiveness and compassion for my parents, and even for my abusers, in order to free myself of the burden I had carried for too long. My relationship with my parents is the healthiest it's ever been, but it is not perfect. I've had to learn how to exist with my mother's ongoing addiction, but I know she's proud of me because she sees that I am choosing a different path from the rest of our family. And although I can't save her or my family, I have saved myself and because of that, maybe I have saved the family that I may go on to have in the future, as I hope they will not not bear the same traumas. Since this rebirth, my life has been a commitment to this healing process and evolution, and it's important to me that I witness others in their own journeys. Although my life is beautiful, it is not perfect because true beauty is flawed. I am still learning how to have healthy relationships and how to re-frame the world I live in, to believe that it can be a safe place. I am still learning how to have healthy boundaries, I am always challenging the urges to self-abandon, to numb and allow dangerous people into my life. My recovery is not a long, straight line. I am still learning how to release myself of the burden that it is my responsibility to save not only my mother, but everyone else. To learn how to witness pain in others without carrying it as my own, and to learn to enjoy my own happiness even when the world around me is suffering.

If I stay on this path and stay committed to myself, I will live a beautiful life, even despite the dark times, despite the mistakes and the slip ups. Healing is not about doing everything right or always being good, staying happy and never feeling pain. Healing is pain. Healing is stepping into old behaviours and recognising it. Healing is showing up as your ugliest, most flawed and frightened self and owning it. It is combining your darkness with your light and honouring both. Healing is showing up however you are in this moment, not showing up as your polished self or how someone else wants you to be. I know that if I am to live a long life, I will die and be reborn many times, and I will bear the fruits of that process and continue to evolve.

The End, and Back to the Beginning
by Jessica Lote

I am Spring. I give you a cold breeze, but it will make you feel alive. Pink, purple, blue, red and yellow flowers are ready to bloom. I represent hope and new beginnings. I allow life to be reborn for a fresh slate after a long cold winter. The grass is clean and reborn again. Trees leaves no longer fall and are green once again. Birds sing as the cycle of life begins anew.

I am Summer. Some hate me and some love me. I am unpredictable. Some days are cold in my season, other days it is as if you're in a volcano. Everything blooms when I come around. I cause your hay fever, your constant need for air conditioning. I am a killer and healer. Life is healthy when I'm present and everything is at its peak, but I am also a killer as the grass dies out and everything becomes dry. Sometimes, life struggles to cope due to the still heat in the atmosphere. I confuse life. Many claim to hate me but travel away during winter to escape the cold. Life complains when it's too hot, life complains when it's too cold, but happiness blooms most this time of year. I see more happening in the world. Life has much more activity and involvement, most commonly at the beach. I am summer. I come and go. When I leave, I am the most missed season of all. I make life worthwhile.

I am Autumn. Also known as Fall, my favourite colour is orange - you will see it everywhere this time of year. Many think of me as the prettiest time of year and I am largely celebrated. The leaves of trees turn orange once again and fall to the ground, leaving it a slippery mess. I have one of the most favoured holidays named Halloween, where people grow pumpkin gardens, dress up as unusual spooky things, and go trick or treating. Those who do not enjoy Summer's company thank me, as I am a colder season, but neutral as I do not cause life to freeze. I bring good feelings, rainy days, warm jumpers and hot chocolate. Life slowly dies, ready for a rebirth after winter.

I am Winter, the most dangerous and miserable season of all. I am a killer. I am loved, if I make it snow, although I often choose not to, especially at Christmas time. After that, I settle in and make life harder. Life is most depressive in this tiring time. There is no life. Flowers are dead, tree life ceases to exist, and land is frozen. Wildlife stores their meals and hide away hibernating until the cold death is over. Millions die in my season, but I have no sympathy as natural selection takes its choosing. I believe in survival of the fittest and that newer life will take over - soon it will be Spring again anyway. The end, and back to the beginning.

The Flames
by Georgia Miles

I met her in the Eastgrove, in the shadows of the Amethyst Spines, just south of the hamlet. Eyes like the sweetest plums, picked ripe from walled gardens to be savoured in the dead of night. This was not our first meeting, to dance where no eyes would stare, to lay upon the lush grass and dream, to submerse ourselves in the cool, moonlit bathed lake. A balm for our seared skin.

She was in my every dream, asleep or awake. Her eyes, her lips, her laughter. That sound she bit back and caged behind her hand during the day became a chorus of wild birds, serenading each other into the night. I have always known I was hers, to start with I was her friend, then her person, then her love. A love that could only be by the shroud of Mother Night or hidden within an invisible moment from the world's clock.

The night was still young as she greeted me with arms so tight and lips so soft. This time was ours. It did not matter that in the morning my mother would berate me for the dark circles under my eyes, undesirable she would say. Undesirable was something I was, to all but my love. Yet this night would not be one of joy, full of whispered words of a life far from this place, a cottage of our own, surrounded by red camellia and chrysanthemums, purple heliotropia and snow-white yarrow. Tonight, we would spot the torches and farmer's pitchforks. Tonight, I would grab her and tell her to run. Tonight, I would watch her go, the forest shifting to hide her path. Their hands were angry, filled with finally released fury, I was now all they despised. I, who had grown up walking the same paths, speaking to the same people, working the same fields, was now something they had never seen but always feared. A monster.

I did not fight as they dragged me back to town, with cheers at the iron clamped around my wrists. My eyes remained on the forest, of the place that had once been our safety. Now the forest mourned, its tree branches bowing, its leaves darkening, for it knew the beauty it had veiled was now marred by impure hands. My fate now judged, they locked me away, guarded by the biggest of their farm boys, till their sacrificial altar was complete.

Movement made my bindings cling like teacups, those farm boys glancing at me with unease, but I was not going anywhere. These manacles were made by slowly trained hands, no need for such things till this fear creeped through the town like a plague. The shed they threw me in once belonged to a family of pigs. All slaughtered. To feed those not starving. I leant my head back against the creaking wood walls, my eyes skyward, through a crack in the roof, the culprit of the gathered puddle to my left. But, through it, I could see the moon. Our moon. The curve of its light gave me a comfort many in this town would never understand and that's when I felt it. Her. The pressure of her head resting on my shoulder, the brush of her flowing hair against my neck, the tenderness of her hand as it played with mine. Yet I knew she was not here. The door had not moved. My eyes would have found her on instinct, yet I felt her.

That voice, a balm to the grooves rubbed into my wrists and the ache of my body from hitting this spot I now resided in.

"My love, I see you."

"But I do not see you."

"Our moon is gracious; she has given me passage to you this night."

"Our last night."

My own voice was smaller than when I had called with conviction that I had been alone in that clearing. Maybe for her I knew what it was to be brave? But now, now their fear had infected me in a different way. Not a fear of what they hunt, but a fear of what they do once they ensnare them. My life was forfeit; my soul knew it the moment I told her to run. Even as the fear of oblivion shook my hands and released the damn in my eyes, I knew one thing for certain; I would do it all again.

My eyes fell from the moon to the dried straw and dirt clinging to my boots. I no longer felt her head upon my shoulder, I no longer felt her hair against my neck, but her hands. Her hands were now cupping my face. Her thumbs, one scarred from a knife slip when she was ten, cast aside my tears. Her voice resolute and unwavering.

"I will not let your soul be wasted for their injudicious fear. Allow the flames to take you my love and I shall remake you into a creature no flames can destroy..."

Her lips met mine, that plum sweetness, a sugary promise. A promise had been our making. Would it be so again? But now, as the shed door scraped across the floor, hands grabbing at my frame, forcing me to stand and follow, I knew she would not forsake me.

A wooden beam met my spine, my arms yanked backwards, secured around it. This poor tree, cut down to be my death sentence. I spoke a soft apology for its sacrifice while my fingertips brushed its coarse bark. Once again, another fate decided without choice. The man this town called leader was speaking, voice booming to the masses, summoning them to chant and call for my death, to save their children and their crops. I saw in the crowd the eyes of my mother, filled with tears. But were they for me, or her? Would they turn on her next? Since is it not that the apple does not fall far from the felled tree? Her fate, it seemed, was undecided or at least not currently under discussion. My eyes found the moon once more as the bellowing man dramatically snatched a torch from the crowd. My death a mere spectacle, a one night only performance.

I knew he wanted my attention as he barked up at me, telling me of all my heathen ways and if I would like to beg his imaginary man for forgiveness. His face grew as red as the roiling flames he carried as my only response was nothing. His deaf ears would not hear me anyway. My fate was sealed but at least she was safe and, somehow, I would be with her again.

He threw down the catalyst to my demise and all watched as it raced through timber and kindling, to meet material and flesh. I, whose voice many here could already not remember, every note I could create coalesced into a cry as those flames pushed aside and burrowed under my skin. The trees bound with me upon this fate cried too, their screeches weaving with my own to become something new. But new sound became something so much more, a sound that turned the audience's fear to terror. A laugh. I was laughing as the fire now licked at my skin like a loving pup, loyal with undying devotion. The body I had been born with was changing more rapidly than my whole twenty years. My skin hardening, my nails elongating, my lips pulling back into a pointed sharp smile as my bonds fell to my feet.

I listened as the air that had once been filled with my screams became polluted with theirs. A cacophony of sublime horror. These fragile beings, they clung to fire to save them from their nightmares, but what is fire - to a dragon.

The Last Breath
by Katrina Stage

The white paint on the window frame is chipping. The sky is grey, and a forceful wind is trying to slip in. It's cold in here. Bone-chilling. I'm sitting on the floor, knees to my chest, next to the worn green blanket I got from my grandma ages ago. It's a rough knit, just the way I like it. Somehow, even the wooden wall is cold against my back. My chest falls as I let out a breath. I rest my tired head on my knee. How did I get here?

He's in the kitchen humming. I still haven't decided if it's a bad habit or something he genuinely enjoys. I would settle for the first. If only I could have a glimpse inside his mind, everything would be so much easier. An open book, a room with no walls. Freedom. But there he is, imperfect, a human being, not designed for margins and rules, no boundaries, no…

A fallen leaf flies past the window. I will never see it again, and even if I do, I will never know it's the same one. Ever. The old door creaks open as a laugh slips out of me.

"Are you okay?" he asks as he walks towards me. My head turns in his direction, my lips in a thin line again.

"Yes," I whisper.

He passes me and puts a mug of tea on the windowsill.

"Thanks."

He crouches down. Such a small gesture becomes bigger in the wrong mind. It's an invasion of personal space, yet it shouldn't be. We have lived here together for months. I invited this man to my house.

"Are you sure you are okay?" he smiles briefly, only one corner of his mouth moving up.

I look deeply at him, digging beyond his eyes, his skull, and his brain until all I can see is the wall and window behind him.

"Yes," I say, still unable to see him, "I'm okay. A bit tired perhaps."

His lips purse.

"You have been sitting here for hours. I made breakfast ages ago. French toast, your favourite."

My vision blurs, and I see him again. All the optimism in the world couldn't convince me he was a happy man. The circles under his eyes, the slight dark stubble, the worn look in his eyes. Am I really that difficult to be with?

"I will get up soon," I smile at him. Insincere. He knows it.

My wandering eyes drift to the window again. There's nothing to look at there. He gets up slowly and leaves the room without saying another word. He even closes the door, something he struggles with immensely.

"I'm sorry."

Am I killing him? Slowly but surely? Am I killing myself? Do I even know how to love without leaving or being left? What is love without hurt, without horrible trauma? How do I make it stop? How do I?

The night settles in, and the wind has vanished. The tea he left stopped steaming hours ago. I heard a car pull out of the driveway. I never heard it come back. So this is it. I'm all alone in this house. It's like I'm sitting in the ruins of some glorious battlefield. The truth is, I'm in this beautiful, old house, well-preserved and loved until I moved in. I had a plan, so many plans. I did, I looked, I organised, I cleaned, I built, I planted, I grew. I stopped. I started thinking.

Cruel contractions of shivers overtake my body. My fingers

are frozen stiff. I need to get the blanket. I reach out for it. I pat the floor until my palm lands on its softness. Why didn't I wrap it around myself hours ago? Why didn't I get up and light the fire? So many questions and so many variables. So many things and knots, words and feelings. The car pulls back into the driveway. Silence falls again. My eyes drop shut. Is this the right time to start praying?

The door flies open, and the light flickers on.

"It's enough," he whispers before wrapping his arms around my cold body and picking me up.

Salt streams flood my cheeks, but no sound escapes my lips. My body is not a body, just a jumble of convulsions and desperation.

"Please," I finally whisper, "Let me go."

His grip becomes tighter for a second before he lowers me onto the sofa. I melt into its surface as we become one and the same. I cease to exist as me. He kneels on the floor beside me, his hand stroking my hair I haven't washed in days.

"Please," I struggle, "Let me be."

His hand drops, and I swallow. The final curtain, it's always close, but you never expect it. He paces back and forth.

If I willed myself to stop breathing, would it happen?

I close my eyes, drifting away from the ceiling. One last breath. Eyelids drop closed. Selfish, needy, too much, too little, too close, too far. Nothing. He wants everything and I can give him nothing. If I willed myself to stop breathing, would it happen?

My eyes dart to the ceiling, and one brief look at him pacing. It's enough. It's time to stop breathing.

The Oak Tree
by Emily Nunan

"Why do we have to live in this creepy house?" Olive cried to her mother. Her mother shooed her away and kept chopping the carrots. The grounds of the property were vast, Olive's mother reminded her not to venture too far by herself. But it was too late.

The sun was shining, Olive shaded her eyes. She heard a giggle by a large oak tree. A pale girl was swinging on a branch.
  "Come and play," the girl giggled.
  Olive climbed high into the tree. A hand clutched her. She tumbled to the ground, no other girl to be seen.

TIMELESS
BY MYA IP

My most inner thoughts align the horizon
To touch, to feel, to kiss
Trapped heavens fall upon: everlasting
The mysteries that await no longer, and yet pray for tomorrow
White feathers grace the floor once more
Timeless
In all forms, the world spins – each year a new story
Never a memory gone to spare
Patience and time to allow for a new journey
Serenity from earth, for mind
Timeless

XVII
by Roan Westall

At dawn and dusk, we saw the first lies of Venus.
Mistaken for a star, a planet like our own,
Though scorching and close to The Sun.
A heavenly body, a god amongst men,
Our magmatic fellow,
Shrouded and suffocating.
He was self-luminous, so we basked in his light.
His distance was unfounded, prophesied secluded,
But his light shone closer than foretold.
Pleasant or passionate, tender or lascivious,
Our dream of divine affinity,
The Morning Star.

A Letter To Myself
by Davinia Ridgwell

First off, it won't be easy - there will be many times when you'll want to quit. But your friends and family will stop you. Life is going to come at you with multiple attacks, and you won't be able to block most of them- heck, maybe not even any. There will be days where waking up is too much as is eating or drinking. There will be days that are simply slept away, never to be experienced.

Some would say these days are wasted, and that you're lazy. Wrong. You're taking time out for yourself. You're finding your ground and the energy to move on. You're fighting the battle, and so far? You're winning.

You're 28 now, 28 with a loving boyfriend and a great group of friends. Friends that you know have your back no matter what. It was a struggle, and it still is - but we did it.

THE PRODUCTION TEAM

COMMISSIONING EDITOR – Eden Sharp

PROJECT MANAGER (Content) - Emmy Johansson

PROJECT MANAGER (Promotion) - Emily Nunan

PUBLICATION

EDITORS - Megan Goff | Shannon Oliver

PUBLISHING ASSISTANT - Nick George

COVER DESIGNER - Carmen Buckley

PUBLICITY

LAUNCH MANAGER - Antoni Bignell-Bird

PROMOTION - Mya Ip | Roan Westall

VIDEO CONTENT CREATORS - Erica Foster | Nick George

MEET THE AUTHORS

ALEXANDRA ALLEN-SMITH

Alexandra graduated from Solent University in 2019. Alexandra plans events at a local castle bringing it to life for the community and also helps couples bring their wedding dreams to life.

GEORGIA AMY

Georgia works as an editor and proofreader after graduating with an MA in English at the University of Plymouth and a BA in English and Creative Writing at Solent University. She loves writing, reading, animals and nature and is currently working on her first novel.

COCO ANN

Aka 'Rockstar Mermaid', Coco graduated from Solent University in 2017 and continued with an MA in Creative Writing. The years of lockdown-imposed self-reflection inspired them to start training as a humanistic psychotherapist. Coco divides their time working with disadvantaged young children and as a volunteer counsellor supporting an LGBTQ+ organisation. They support those dealing with intersectionality and otherness along with a voice for the working class. One of Coco's goals is to provide safe, non-discriminatory counselling and support for sex workers and to help destigmatise and decriminalise sex work.

MARTIN ANSELL

Martin used to think poetry was all like 'nahh mate' but is now all like 'sound mush'.

JORDAN BAND

Jordan graduated from Solent University in 2022. He completed an English Single Honours degree and describes his writing style as a mixture of poetry and ramblings. He is currently studying to be a teacher at the University of Southampton.

He reflects: 'My time at Solent gave me so many skills and memories that I will carry through my life'.

ANTONI BIGNELL-BIRD

Antoni returns from his university hiatus to retake his second year. Despite taking the scenic route to graduation, he feels honoured to have been part of the publishing team for this final anthology. He used to think that words of wisdom claiming that setbacks are a part of the journey were bullshit, but now that he has experienced several, he begrudgingly admits that they have been the best thing to ever happen to him. Antoni is now determined to prove that the best pace to work in is your own.

His submission was late by a week and two days.

LASMA BRAUKE

Lasma graduated from Solent University in 2019 and is now living in Latvia and happily reminiscing about her studies, filled with literary art and inspiration. She likes to write poetry about the issues of her personal life and society.

'If it's hard to talk about it, you can always rhyme about it.'

HOLLY-MAY BROADLEY-DARBY

Holly-May is currently studying English and Creative Writing at Solent University and has a passion for writing. She currently has one novel published.

CARMEN BUCKLEY

Carmen is a queer writer and illustrator who specialises in writing about the downtrodden; communities that are often looked down upon in society. She wishes to give them a voice through her dark and character-driven storytelling, yet also bring a sense of hope into this messed-up world.

AMY BUTLER

Amy is a Solent University English Literature & Creative Writing alumni and she continues to write passionately.

ABIGAIL-JANE CHAMPION

Abigail-Jane is an aspiring writer, currently navigating life's ups and downs and documenting the experience along the way.

ABBY COOMBES

Water and feed daily. Do not place in direct sunlight. Keep in a warm, dry place. Benefits from being placed where there is a steady flow of fresh air.

POPPY CROSSFIELD

Poppy is a Solent University English graduate from the Kentish coast. She is currently writing her first novel, a combination of the works of Anne Rice and Roman mythology, when she is not gaming with her husband or otherwise chasing after their son.

SHANNON FEAVER

Shannon is an Acting and Performance student with a love for writing fiction as a hobby, more specifically thriller and horror. She has a love for all things creative and artful and wants to inspire others to dive into literature and any other kind of art.

ERICA FOSTER

Erica is a writer who loves dark fantasy
and equally dark humour.

NICK GEORGE

Fascinated with the art of communication and storytelling, Nick gets a thrill from working with words both professionally and for pleasure. During her marketing career she delivered PR, copywriting and content for many organisations from start-ups to blue chip companies. She also spent three years as features editor for a national sports magazine.

Nick enjoys manipulating words to evoke emotion and spur action, and aspires to teach English alongside ongoing copywriting and fiction-writing ventures.

MEGAN GOFF

Megan was a witch in a past life. She now studies English and Creative Writing at Solent University, and enjoys writing and reading in her spare time.

She slayed as an editor.

MILES HERON

Born in rainy England, Miles spent his time inside. On those days, his family gazed outside, sighed, and crossed a mental tally for another day wasted. In the head of Miles, however, deadly strangers with black cats squatted.

These thoughts have escaped into anthologies *Moonlight* and *Limbo,* available on Amazon, and he feels 'honoured and privileged' to have been able to contribute to this final anthology.

ELI HILL

Eli is a queer, disabled poet who refuses to consume any sad media but cries during the creation of every single piece of their own work.

Recently more used to the clinical starkness of medical settings than the lyricism and beauty of poetry, Eli draws upon their unique blend of experiences to write poems that help them to express the complexity of their emotions. When not occupied by writing or their entire body falling apart at the seams, Eli can usually be found crocheting or reading around any number of topics, always eager to learn something new.

MYA IP

An English and Creative Writing student who also works as a teaching assistant, training for her dream job; a teacher. Mya's desire to help future generations came from her secondary school English teacher who said there are many ways of helping others, and to do so as a career is something truly special.

Mya's passion is to write romance and fantasy stories, and publishing a book about life and death has been a new challenge which she has loved experimenting with. While completing her DofE award, Mya stepped out of her comfort zone adapting to a new approach to working. She feels this helped her to relate to and explore different themes for this anthology.

GEORGIA JERREY

Now an English teacher, Georgia continues to write in her free time since her time at Solent University studying English and Creative Writing. She enjoys inspiring the next generation of creative writers.

In 2021 she published a poem anthology *Through the Seasons* with Bookleaf Publishing and hopes for many more works to come, including *My Dear Mistress* and *Island Syrena*.

EMMY JOHANSSON

'With freedom, books, flowers and the moon, who could not be happy?' – *Oscar Wilde*

YNA LAZARTE

Yna (whose actual name is Jan-Yna, but never question why she's named that) is a Filipina, and a closet geek who is sometimes curious about most things in life- maybe too curious. Her guilty pleasures include baked and grilled goods, cacti, video games, anime and indie music.

ROSIE LEWIS

Rosie was a fleeting Solent University student from 2018-20. Eclectic, erratic creator spewing words for her own entertainment.

'It's a pleasure to have been asked to contribute to this glorious tribute to the English Collective and the entirety of the English department. Thank you to all our amazing lecturers who have worked so hard for all of us students, past and present. Each one of you has left a mark on our souls - we wouldn't be the writers that we are without knowing you.'

AMIE LOCKWOOD

After graduating from Solent University in 2017, Amie did an exhilarating stint in fast food pizza before becoming a proofreader and content creator for a digital marketing agency in the West Country. Currently uncertain what they really want to do with their life (apart from playing rugby), they are travelling the globe and meeting inspiring people. Their writing draws on some very personal thoughts, challenges and experiences, as well as influences and stories from people they've met.

JESSICA LOTE

Jessica studies English and Creative Writing at Solent University. She dreams of publishing a novel she has been thinking about for years, and being a best-selling writer and also enjoys writing music. Jessica's genres and themes of writing are violence, protest, dystopian, and despair with a chance of hope and change. Jessica's writing is dark and contains subliminal messages, and hopes her literature will inspire change.

Her goal is having a dream house in the middle of nowhere, by the fire, book in hand, or with her laptop typing out her next piece of work.

LAURA MASON

Laura graduated with Solent's English Literature and Creative Writing degree in 2017. Since then, her career has led to work in the education publishing sector, where she is a project editor at City & Guilds. She still writes as frequently as she can, as much as her elderly laptop allows her to.

CHLOE MCBEATH

Chloe is a past English Literature student at Solent University. During her time at Solent, Chloe had a short story *Everlast* published in *Myriad* by The English Collective. She went on to work in the care industry during the pandemic, and now has a career in optics. With her passion for poetry and encouragement from writer friends, Chloe continues to explore the literary world.

GEORGIA MILES

Now in the final year of a course she doesn't want to end, Georgia Miles has learnt so much from the lecturers of the English and Creative Writing course at Solent University.

An aspiring writer and playwright, she hopes that readers will enjoy her work and find their own voices represented.

BILLIE-MARTHA NEWLAND

Billie studied English and Creative Writing, graduating in 2022. They like to write tragic poetry relating to loss, in hope that it helps others overcome the pain of grief and suffering. Billie ha a love for Wicca and Reiki; practising daily meditation to clear their mind and take care of their mental health. Their favourite author is HP Lovecraft and favourite poet is Sylvia Plath. Billie studied during the Covid years and suffered the loss of many loved ones which is where they got their poetry inspiration.

EMILY NUNAN

Emily is a passionate person who enjoys writing fiction and loves when others read her work even if it is absurd and based on murdering people with bread. Enjoyment or hatred from reading her writing is something she inspires to create, so happy reading.

SHANNON OLIVER

Shannon is currently studying English and Creative Writing. She aspires to be a full-time author and to write her own fantasy series. She also intends to become a publisher due to her love of reading. Shannon enjoys reading fiction of all genres set all over the world and hopes to one day write novels focusing on minorities to provide different groups in society with the representation they have lacked for years.

JESSICA PAIGE

Since graduating in 2019, Jessica has worked in journalism and copywriting. The skills she learnt and interests she discovered at Solent University are aiding in her career today, especially when it comes to her passion for accessibility and inclusivity.

DAVINIA RIDGWELL

Hai hai hai, the name's Dee. I was a student from 2016 to 2019 and I loved it! Such a wonderful course and it had the best tutors, a major shame it's ending. I still write when I've got free time, but being an assistant manager at Hollywood Bowl Basingstoke, does mean it's scarce.

I've been self-published and officially published, both stories and poems, and I'm still working on many, many book ideas as I can't stick to just one. But listen, don't let this sway you from being the writer you wish to be.

Life is all about taking chances and risks to reach those dreams people tell you are impossible, so grab that pen and notepad and get creating. The only true obstacle standing in the way is yourself!

EDEN SHARP

Proud nurturer of the English Collective 2014-2023.
Lecturer, English and Creative Writing.
Crime thriller author.

'There will always be fertile soil. There will always be the genius seed inside you. There will always be the opportunity to combine the two.' – *David Ault*

KATRINA STAGE

Katrina is a former student of English and Creative Writing but forever a student of literature and searcher for the meaning of what she refers to as 'this stupid, slightly messed up life'.

DAPHNE VAN HOOLWERFF

An English-Dutch translator from the Netherlands, Daphne currently lives in Southampton. She studied Journalism in her home country before travelling to the UK to complete an MA in Creative Writing, and taking part in the English programme at Solent University as an exchange student. Reading and writing are ongoing passions and hobbies in her life.

HOLLIE WARD

Since graduating Hollie has worked as a spoken word poet and a writing and drama coach, and is now a marketing executive.

She taught the Mayflower Young Writers at The Mayflower Theatre, focusing on creative writing and community performance. She has also delivered reading intervention programmes and Wessex Schools Poetry Slam workshops in schools, as well as sessions in voice projection, public speaking, reader reception and *King Lear*. Hollie's performance history includes Hampshire Reclaim the Night, Riverfest, the Romsey TeaPoet Collective, Word Makers and Silence Breakers. Also as a sacrificial poet at Hammer & Tongue National Finals at the Royal Albert Hall. She was published in *The Writers Desk* and awarded The Festival Scholarship for Winchester Writers' Festival in 2018.

CARLIE WELLS

Currently studying English Literature and Creative Writing at Solent University, Carlie aspires to be an English teacher. From a young age, her parents encouraged both reading stories and writing them, a passion that has never stopped, only growing each day.

ROAN WESTALL

Author. Poet. Musician. Wizard.

THE GARDEN OF EDEN

All goes onward and outward - nothing collapses.
  - *Walt Whitman*

And so it goes.
  — *Kurt Vonnegut*

Printed in Great Britain
by Amazon